WELCOME TO COTTONWOOD CREEK

COMPILED BY THOMAS BAKER

Copyright © 2019 by 6K Press

All rights reserved. This book or any portion thereof may not be reproduced or used in any manner whatsoever without the express written permission of the publisher except for the use of brief quotations in a book review.

Printed in the United States of America

www.6kpress.com

DEDICATION

Huge thanks to not only the great writers who contributed to this project but to everyone who has supported our ideas and been there for us all! It's an incredible and humble feeling to share a love to create with so many great people!

Don't ever let anyone discourage your creative drive.

Special thanks to Robert for helping keep this anthology running and piecing the puzzle together! We will do our best to keep this train rolling full speed, all aboard The 6K Press Express! Next stop, Cottonwood Creek.

Enjoy!

-Thomas Baker

CONTENTS

Aaron Thorton	Welcome	1
Thomas Baker	Cottonwood Creek	3
Robert Wagner	New to Town	13
Jonathan Edward Ondrashek	Severed Attachments	39
Thomas Baker	Do You Know the Muffin Man?	59
David Owain Hughes	Jany-Jay Does a Duet	65
Maxine Grey	The Vessel	75
Aaron Thorton	Pure Schitt Luck	81
Thomas Baker	Night School	97
Caitlin Geer	Rear View Mirror	105
David Owain Hughes	Caution Slippery When Wet	113
Thomas Baker	Settling In	125
Jonathan Edward Ondrashek	Uncaged	131
Thomas Baker	Midnight Cruise	151
David Owain Hughes	Daddy Stitch	159
Robert Wagner	The Saga of John Elton	161
Thomas Baker	Burial Ground Buchery	189

WELCOME

By Aaron Thorton

I feel cold as the night when the long road ended
Sticky as the spot where I laid your head down
Muddy as the water where I washed my hands of you
Broken as the girl cuz she cut my heart in two
I fear perdition's coming on...
But no one ever comes to The Cottonwood Creek
On account of the leeches and the horrible stink
So I lay your head down...
Lay your head down by the water to sleep...
I feel bent as the crippled man twisting in his sleep
As empty as the devil who stole my soul
Crouched in the corner of The Cottonwood Creek
With the rats and the fishes and the secrets they keep...
Oh no, perdition's coming strong...
Pale as the moon that snatched my shadow I feel as haunted as a guilty man...
But no one ever comes to The Cottonwood Creek...

WELCOME TO COTTONWOOD CREEK

COTTONWOOD CREEK

"Cottonwood Creek? Yeah, fuck that!" Omarr exclaimed from the backseat when JD and Gravy brought up the idea of heading to the local myth filled badland to drink around a surely rough shot attempt at a bonfire.

Omarr's reaction brought laughter to Tom, who sat next to him in the back of Gravy's old navy blue Cutlass Supreme, which was more affectionately known to most as The Gravy Boat!

JD had just gotten of work when the other three picked him up. After that they headed to his Aunt's liquor store, where they grabbed up a couple of cases of beer, and drove off with no particular destination in mind.

The four of them traveled many miles around town on a normal basis but tonight they headed to drink and relax. That's when Gravy brought up the idea of cruising out to Cottonwood Creek. They knew all the stories, both the facts and the legends of the place. One fun fact was the guy who killed his girlfriend by drowning her in the creek. He left her lying there, with her head in the water, and he drove off, never to be seen again. The most legendary and terrifying tale was the alleged Crippled Man, who haunted the area. A local mythological creature of sorts, supposedly responsible for several missing persons and limitless nightmares. To some, mainly young high school age kids, the creek was a place to come park, make out, and hopefully get laid. That was before the stench of the place took over on most warm days, not to mention anyone who went in the water came out caked in leeches.

"Come on Omarr don't be a puss!" JD shot to the backseat, clearly poking fun at him. "You scared The Crippled Man is going to get ya?" The prodding earned JD the middle finger.

The Crippled Man was more of the myth variety of Cottonwood, rumor had it that if you went down to the creek on a bright, moonlit night, you would see a twisted, crippled man lurking in the shadows, surrounded by rats. If he saw you, you felt like you were tied up and drowning without ever being in the water. When you eventually passed out, The Crippled Man would steal your soul.

"I ain't afraid of no ghosts!" Omarr eventually exclaimed from the back seat. "Besides. I know I'm faster than you. So I should be fine."

"Fat jokes, Omarr has fat jokes!" JD laughed from the passenger seat, along with the other three guys in the car.

WELCOME TO COTTONWOOD CREEK

Gravy took a right turn onto the old gravel road that led down to the creek. The Cutlass rolled to a stop near one of the chained off paths that would take them to their destination. The city officials had made a few feeble attempts to try and keep people out or away from the creek, but none of them lasted or ever seemed to work.

Tom led the four of them down the loosely packed path toward the water with a flashlight, JD and Omarr followed. JD with the beer, Omarr with some chairs. Gravy brought up the rear after retrieving his acoustic guitar and a plastic grocery bag full of items to burn, and more important, to get the fire started. They set up the chairs and made a crude circle of rocks for the fire. JD and Tom ventured off with the flashlight to grab some wood while Gravy and Omarr got all the other stuff ready.

It wasn't long before the four friends plopped down in their seats around the growing glow of the flames, beers in hand. The four buddies sat around shooting the shit as they tossed back one brewski after another. For nearly three hours they mainly bitched about their jobs,bragged about the the chicks who had allegedly graced their beds and regaled one another with tales of things they had heard or experienced at the creek.

Gravy was as entertaining as always with his guitar. The guy may have only knew a few riffs from a hundred different songs, but the fucking dude played them well! After the gang made a horrible attempt at harmonizing vocals of a Bon Jovi classic, Tom checked his watch. That's when realized they had been there much later than he had planned. He had to be at work in a few short hours. He told his compadres he had to get ready to head home and Gravy agreed, which of course meant the party was over for everyone. No one really complained, as the beer was running low and warm now anyhow.

JD was the first to volunteer to carry stuff up to the car, telling everyone he had to piss anyways. He grabbed up the last open case of beer, his chair, and headed up the hill to the car. The other three guys stomped out the fire and covered it with dirt before they headed towards the path themselves, chairs in hand. Omarr carried the flashlight, even though the moon lit the way in a perfect white light.

As Omarr crest the top of the hill, he looked back, puzzled. "Maybe I drank more than I realized, but is this not where we parked the car?"

Gravy and Tom joined his side, both also looked a bit befuddled, until Tom broke the puzzled silence. "Funny JD", he yelled. "Come on guy, you know we have to go!" There was no response.

WELCOME TO COTTONWOOD CREEK

"Uhh, dude." Gravy muttered as he dangled his car keys from his index finger.

"Wait, if you have the keys, then how the hell did he move the car? I mean come on, we all know how JD likes to fuck with people." Tom commented.

He clicked on the flashlight and scanned the area. There was no sign of JD or the car anywhere. The three guys stood there in the eerie silence of the moonlight, feeling at a complete loss of what in the hell was going on.

"Look." Gravy finally broke the quiet moment. "Here's the plan. We set our shit down here and walk up the road and see where the fuck my car is and where JD's drunk ass has wandered off to."

Omarr and Tom agreed. They piled their stuff up and headed down the road, using the flashlight to check both sides. They walked about a half mile up the road when they heard some old timey guitar playing from behind them. Gravy got pissed, he didn't like people touching Sara, his beloved guitar. He led the charge as they headed back where they had started. Upon getting there all their stuff was gone, well not gone as much as moved.

"Yeah, I'm pretty sure it's time to go," Omarr said as he pointed back down the hill toward the part of the creek bed where they had hung out.

Their chairs were sat back up. The fire had reignited. Gravy's guitar burned in the middle of it. In a rage Gravy rushed down the hill and kicked his smoldering instrument out of the fire. It landed on the pebbled ground and broke into several charred and blackened pieces, too ruined to ever play again.

"JD YOU MOTHERFUCKER!!! COME OUT AND I WILL BEAT YOUR ASS MYSELF!" Fury shook Gravy's voice.

There was no reply, then laughter peeled in the darkened distance. Not your normal laughter, but the cackle of what one could imagine a maniacal movie monster would sound like. Tom and Gravy looked at each other with worry, then looked back to Omarr. He was now gone too.

"Omarr?" Tom said, nervous to ask aloud.

"He came back down with us right?" Gravy no more finished asking the question when a splash in the water made them both jump off the ground.

Tom aimed the flashlight towards the water. They saw nothing at first, then a dark lump floated into view. It bobbed toward the bank. They kept the light trained on it until they realized it was Omarr. He was lifeless, pale, and covered in leeches. He looked as though he had been floating in the water for days. His eyes were open wide with panic.

WELCOME TO COTTONWOOD CREEK

"We have to get the fuck out of here right now! I don't know what in the hell is going on but every part of me says we need to leave." Tom ordered.

Gravy didn't argue, he nodded his head in quiet agreement. The cackle erupted in the darkness again this time followed by the rustle of trees and bushes nearby, as if something was running towards them. Tom and Gravy didn't hesitate, they took off sprinting toward the trail. The beam of the flashlight caught a glimpse of someone standing a few feet away in the trees. It was JD.

"Bro, tell me you're fucking around right now man!" Tom called out but JD didn't respond, he didn't even turn around.

Tom focused the light on him. JD looked as if he was shivering. He handed the light to Gravy and told him to keep it on JD. He started towards his friend. Gravy felt an overwhelming sense of dread as Tom got closer. He twisted the end of the flashlight to widen the amount of light it gave out. Tom stood behind JD, still calling to him and asking if he was ok, with no response at all from him. Tom stepped in close to him and placed his hand on JD's shoulder. In a sudden jerk JD spun. Gravy watched in horror as he plunged what looked like a metal tent stake into Tom's throat. He fell to the ground, gasping for his final breaths. JD stood there staring at him on the ground, then casually turned around and faced back in the same direction.

Gravy shook, riddled with fear. He took off up the trail and nearly fell over himself as he reached the top. His car sat exactly where they had left it. Another loud splash had him whirl around to look back down the hill. JD was gone, so was Tom. Through the fear and adrenaline he ruffled for his keys in his pocket, jumped in the car, started it up, and nearly shit himself as he kicked the headlights on. Omarr and Tom stood in front of his car, like undead statues covered in leeches. He reached for the shifter and cried out when JD lunged forward from the backseat, grabbed his hand, and forced the car into drive. Gravy tried to fight off JD as the car lurched forward, like it was being pushed. JD grabbed the wheel to steer the car over the peak of the hill. Gravy tried to grab the door handle to jump out as the car barreled towards the water, but JD held him too tightly. The car hit the water at one of its widest points and sank. As the water bubbled in and filled the car, Gravy saw him. A crippled looking old man watching the car sink. Smiling and waving as the car submerged into the dark muddy water.

WELCOME TO COTTONWOOD CREEK

JD woke up with a gasp in his chair sitting by the burnt out fire. The sky was turning shades of orange as the sun rose.

"I can't believe those fuckers left me out here."

WELCOME TO COTTONWOOD CREEK

NEW TO TOWN

The jet black van pulled up into the driveway just as the matching clouds over head opened up, dumping down buckets of rain. The driver of the van cursed as he sprinted around the front of the vehicle and down the sidewalk to the covered porch.

"Well that's just great. Now I'm all wet," Justin mumbled to himself as he searched his pocket for the key to his new home.

As he did, Justin looked around his new neighborhood through the torrential downpour. Across the road a home sat way back on the lot. At the end of its long driveway, by the mailbox, stood an older man. It shocked Justin that the man stood there, his eyes seemed cold and uncaring, even from this distance.

The man wore a dingy gray bathrobe that matched the ring of soaked hair that remained on his head. His eyes were laser focused on Justin, oblivious to anything else. Justin knew that as a stranger moving into such a small community, he would get the outsider treatment and prepared for it. He didn't imagine a reaction as extreme as the man across the street.

With the hand not fishing for the house key, Justin waved at the man. The old man continued to stare at him with a dead eyed look. Justin shivered, and not just from his cold, rain soaked clothing.

"I didn't think I was moving in across from a creepy old man from a Stephen King novel." Justin found the key and used it. Grateful to be inside, for more reasons than just escaping the rain, he stood there, listening to himself drip on the hardwood floor.

I'll have to get a rug for the entryway, he thought. He looked around, the staring old men now forgotten. He had lots to do; the moving truck would be there soon. How am I going to not ruin the carpet of my new home?

The next day the skies were clear and Justin went out on the concrete slab in his backyard, taking a break in a lawn chair. Beside him on a small glass table sat a cold beer. He let out a sigh of content. The decision to move out of the city and into the countryside was the right one. The view and the smells were much better.

Across his large, open back yard laid the yard of his neighbor's house. They had a two story house, unlike his single story one. A deck attached to the

WELCOME TO COTTONWOOD CREEK

back of the house, under which was a concrete patio with sliding glass doors that led to the inside.

The glass door slid back as he looked over the house and a pretty young woman emerged. She looked in her mid twenties, with shoulder length light brown hair. The big curls in it bounced as she walked across her lawn.

Justin looked awkwardly away once he realized he was staring. When he looked back, she smiled and waved at him. She walked his way then rubbed her hands on her blue jeans.

"Shit," Justin whispered to himself. He stood up and walked to meet her.

"Hi," the woman said as she took his outstretched hand. Her voice was as pretty as her face, light and fun. Her lips were thin and her teeth filled her mouth as she smiled. "I didn't know the person who bought this place had already moved in."

"Yes he did. I mean I did. Me, Justin." He chuckled.

"Hi Justin. I'm Samantha."

"Nice to meet you, Samantha." Justin was sweating by this point, even though the air held a little fall chill. He told himself to relax.

Samantha shielded her eyes as the sun came from behind a cloud. "Let me be one of the first to welcome you. Where did you move here from?"

"Atlanta. Originally I'm from Omaha. That's in Nebraska."

She giggled. "Yeah. Of course it is."

"Yeah. Right." Justin grinned like a dummy.

"You'll be in shock, I bet, switching gears from the big city to our little town."

"I picked this place because I wanted a change. The big city wasn't doing it for me."

"I hope we do it for you then." Samantha smiled a little wider. "In fact, let me invite you over for dinner tomorrow night. We'll be neighbors after all."

"Don't you have to ask your husband first?" Justin asked. "I wouldn't want to come across as rude if he's not prepared to have a stranger over. I should at least meet him first."

Samantha's smiled dimmed. "He passed away about a year ago. It was sudden. One day here, the next day he was gone."

"I'm sorry about that," Justin said, sounding and feeling like an even bigger dummy. Why didn't I look for a ring? Now that he glanced down, he could see the shadow of where it had been on her finger.

"Thank you and hey, we just met." She shrugged. "How would you have known?" Samantha's perkiness came back. "So Thursday night, say 6:30?"

"Sounds great. I've yet to make a real grocery run anyway."

WELCOME TO COTTONWOOD CREEK

Samantha turned and left. As he watched her walk home, Justin congratulated himself again on moving to Gateway City.

The next day Justin parked at the elementary school and got out. It was an old style, long low brick building. Probably built in the fifties he guessed. It was the only school in town. The middle school and high school were in the next town over, which hosted several towns worth of children in the rural area

The wind blustered as he crossed the mostly empty lot. The chill of fall held a warning in the wind. He spent a good minute searching by the front door for the buzzer to call the office to let him in before it hit him. They didn't have a need for such a thing out here. He tried the door and it opened.

He crossed the small foyer and entered the school office. Inside it was dim and cramped. Behind a long, dark wood counter sat an old lady. Justin immediately had an image of her sitting at a bar holding a smoldering cigarette in one hand and a glass of whiskey in the other. Right now she banged away on an old keyboard in front of a computer monitor that looked like it was from the nineties.

"Can I help you?" she asked in a voice that matched Justin's image in his head. She didn't even look up.

"Hi, I'm Justin. I'm the new teacher for fourth grade. I wanted to check in, say hi to the principal. Get acquainted with the place." He made sure to sound upbeat and cheerful.

"Great," the lady replied. Justin could swear he heard disgust in her voice. "Another new one. Just wait and I'll be with you."

Justin didn't have long to contemplate her weird comment, maybe she meant they had high turnover, as a moment later a man emerged from a dusty door on the wall behind and to the right of the receptionist. He was an average looking middle aged man, except his nose was too long and wide for his otherwise slim face. He grabbed Justin's hand in a smothering grip and gave it three exaggerated pumps.

"Hello. You must be Justin, correct?" The man said, smiling with extraordinarily white teeth as he talked. "I'm Principal Tanner. Let me apologize for Ms. Pierce."

"Go ahead," Ms. Pierce said not stopping her typing as she spoke. "Everyone's been doing it forever."

WELCOME TO COTTONWOOD CREEK

Mr. Tanner gave Justin a knowing look before sweeping an arm in front of him. "Come this way, and we can talk while I show you to your classroom."

Thursday had come and after a day of teaching, Justin went home to change. It had been an easy first couple of days, if a little strange. Everyone welcomed him nice enough, well except for Ms. Pierce. She scowled at him every time she saw him. Which to be fair, she seemed to do to everybody. He also wasn't surprised to learn her first name was Marge.

The rest of the staff he wasn't sure about either. They all seemed strange, something seemed a little off about them. For now Justin was willing to write it off as small down idiosyncrasies. He was the new person in the well knit community and all that.

He stood in front of his closet wondering what he should change into. The button up shirt might be to stuffy and formal but a tee shirt wouldn't cut it. He kept telling himself this wasn't a date but that didn't seem to help with making up his mind.

He ended up going with the nicest long sleeve pullover he had, since when the sun went down the temperature dropped like a rock. He rang the doorbell of Samantha's house, tapping his foot and wondering if he should have brought something with him, like wine. In what seemed like agonizing minutes, she opened the door.

"Hi, Justin. Nice to see you. Come in," Samantha said.

Justin smiled big and walked through the doorway. Standing next to her Justin realized for the first time Samantha was a few inches taller than him. "Thanks for having me over. This way I didn't have to have frozen pizza again."

"Sure," Samantha chuckled.

Justin took a look around as she led him into the dining room. It was a nice place, well maintained. The place was big, he wondered if she felt rattling around in it by herself. He didn't see any pictures of any family or her with her late husband. Maybe she took them all down as it was still to painful? He didn't know. As he walked further in, what he saw of the house made him think maybe she didn't like decorating. Every room was bare, almost spartan.

In the dining room, a nice but simple light brown oak table for two. Samantha gestured for him to sit. "I'll plate it and bring it out."

Feeling a little awkward about all of this, he didn't really even know her, Justin did as she asked. He made some small talk. "This is a nice house you have."

WELCOME TO COTTONWOOD CREEK

"Thank you," she called from the kitchen, which was through an opening to the right of where he sat. "Really, yours is just as nice."

Justin waited until she came back in with a plate in each hand before continuing the conversation. She put down a chicken breast covered in mushroom and a white sauce, with sautéed spinach on the side. Justin felt immediately like this was too much. He wasn't going to complain though.

"Oh, you've been inside my house?" Justin said as Samantha settled into her chair.

"Yes, a few times. The family that lived there before you. They had a daughter. It was sad, what happened."

Justin waited with wonder as he finished chewing his bite. "What happened? Is the place haunted? Is that why the price was so low?" He chucked.

"No, I don't think so," Samantha said. She answered in a tone too serious for his taste. "The little girl, she was only nine, died. The Mom and Dad moved away a week after the funeral."

"Oh." That oh was lame to Justin, but he didn't know what else to say. "I guess my little joke was crass then."

"Well obviously you didn't know," Samantha said between bites. "It's not like the realty company advertised the fact."

"How did she die?" The words leapt out before Justin could stop himself.

"I don't know if you paid much attention to it but there is a large, sort of boggy forest that runs along the highway you take to school. She had somehow gotten over there and had gotten lost. I heard the poor thing was in bad shape when they found her. It looked like wild animals attacked her is what went around town. I never asked, that would be rude."

Justin looked down at his half eaten chicken and put his utensils down. He needed a break from eating, to clear out that mental image. He had no idea the evening would start out so morbid.

Samantha must have read the look on his face. "I'm sorry, I didn't mean to go into gruesome details. That's not very appropriate dinner talk, is it? Why don't you tell me about the last place you lived?"

The rest of the evening they spent in banal small talk. She asked him to stay for a glass of wine, but Justin refused as polite as he could. Not that he didn't want to stay. Once they had shifted from the morbid territory of the previous owners of his house losing their daughter, he had a nice evening and enjoyed her company. He was afraid of pushing what could end up being something too fast. He hadn't even been in town a week, and Samantha could just be a very friendly person. He didn't know her yet, and he didn't want to get ahead of himself and look a fool.

With a huge grin on his face, he walked back into his house. The lights were all off. Where before the darkness didn't bother him, now it seemed heavy and foreboding. He flicked the switch and the full darkness retreated into shapely shadows cast by his living room furniture. He sat down on his couch instead of heading up to bed like he should have. School would start early in the morning.

Justin drove home in the dark. Brown leaves swirled around his headlights as he drove home. A thin fog hugged the highway.

He hated that he had been stuck at the school late. It was Friday night for one thing. For another had plans for Samantha to come over to his house and he still needed to pick up. He had been a lax bachelor lately for no reason other than laziness.

The Mazda Three purred along at about ten miles over the speed limit. His mind wasn't on the road when the little girl flashed in front of his lights. He had just enough time to register that she had long straight black hair and wore a purple polka dot dress.

"Holy shit!" Justin stomped on the brake, feeling the vibration up into this leg. He found himself in battle with the wheel to stay on the road. In one instant the girl stood in front of him and the next she wasn't there.

The screeching of tires still echoed in his mind as he got out and smelt the burnt rubber. He legs felt like rubber as he walked towards the back of his car. He didn't want to see what he had done.

"Oh man. Oh hell. Oh man," he repeated over and over again as he squinched his eyes, preparing as much as he could to see the damage.

He walked and with each step the mist rolled around his pant legs. He felt sure he would've seen her body by now. With a shiver passing through his body, he stopped and turned around. The car became a white figure in the gathering fog. "What the hell?"

Then he had a terrible thought. What if she had gotten caught up under the car? He raced back and dropped to the ground, scraping up his hands in the process. No, there was nothing under his car.

Justin stood back up and wiped the road grime from his slacks. "I did see a girl right? I mean, I don't know what a child would be doing out on the road, at night, in the fog, but still..."

He walked towards the back of his car again when he heard the sound of snapping branches from the forest that crowded the road to his right. The sounds of the creatures of the night, which he didn't notice till now had stopped, creaked and chirped once more. Like the snap brought them back from whatever hiding places his squealing tires had driven them into.

"Hello?" Justin called out. Could he have thrown her into the woods?

He walked with hesitant steps to the tree line. He examined the ground, trying to find a place where it looked like an object might have broken through. The increasing fog made it hard for him to see into the forest. "Hello?" he called again, louder this time.

Cracking noise straight ahead of him made his hairs on his arms stand up. The thin hoodie he had on suddenly didn't seem enough to keep the chill out. Justin stood frozen, not knowing what to do? He really didn't want to go into the woods at night. The story that Samantha had told him about finding the chewed up body of a child in there came to mind. But he knew it wasn't right to drive off without finding the kid he had hit.

Against all his better judgment Justin went back to his car. He grabbed the tiny flashlight out of the glove box. When he stood back up, that's when he noticed the front of the car. It didn't have a scratch or dent on it. He got closer, examined it with the flashlight, and still couldn't find any evidence that he had hit anything.

"Hello?" he almost screamed, shutting up the sounds of the night again. Justin strained his ears. All he heard was the rubbing of branches in the slight breeze that had picked up.

Justin thought he saw something move at the edge of his flashlight, out behind the trees. He shivered and decided it was time to go. He got back in behind the wheel, locked the doors, and with a rush of held breath, put the car in drive.

Justin had gone straight home, thinking he would forget all about the weird occurrence that happened on the way. Instead, he opened the door to his house, saw all that darkness yawning before him, and called up Samantha.

Now here he sat on her couch in the cool, white lights of electrical reality. He felt more foolish as the story went on until at the end he was afraid his face was flushed.

She restored some dignity to him with her question. "Would you be surprised to hear you're not the first person to see things down around Murlak Creek woods?" Samantha said.

"I'm surprised, all right. Relieved as well, if I'm honest. I thought maybe all these years with the kids had finally driven me over the edge. It's a teacher thing, you heard of it?"

Samantha giggled, which Justin enjoyed hearing. "I guess that's one of your occupational hazards, huh?" Justin shrugged and grinned. "Seriously, just about everyone in town as seen some shape in the mists coming off the bogs in the forest. My dad told me it had something to do with topography, the way the winds carry across the land here, things like that. Of course us humans are good at putting together patterns out of chaos."

Justin had learned in the past months that Samantha had once moved away for a little while and work as a psychologist before giving it up to come back to Gateway City. Now she held the glamorous job of running the little three aisle grocery store in town. He hadn't had the nerve yet to ask her why she had made such a choice.

"So what it boils down to is that it was all in my head?" Justin tapped his forehead three times.

"Along with everyone else in this town, including me. One time I could swear I saw an elephant charging out of the mist" she said, completely straight faced.

"I think my bullshit meter is going off," Justin said. He stood to leave. "Thanks for having me over. I gotta get to bed, gotta grind the wheel stone again tomorrow."

She stood as well and came over to his side of her kitchen table. She took his hand in hers. "If you are still spooked, you could always stay over here tonight, instead of going back home alone."

Stunned, Justin quickly recovered and smiled. He took her up on that offer.

A very satisfying winter break came and went before Justin knew it. He was getting ready to spend the last night of freedom with Samantha before the back to school crush began.

He was picking her up tonight. The plan was to have a night out in the biggest city close by, which was still about an hour away. It was her request, and Justin was falling for her so hard, he was willing to do whatever she wanted.

WELCOME TO COTTONWOOD CREEK

He made the drive around the winding neighbor that took longer than it did just to walk over to her house. He left the car running as he went up to get her. She opened the door before he even got a chance to ring the doorbell.

"You look great," Justin said. She did, wearing a dark red dress that stopped at her knees and sparkled with every move she made. "I take it you're ready?"

She gave him a smile but something about it seemed reserved. "Let's go."

Justin just assumed he read it wrong and escorted her to his car. She was unusually silent most of the trip to the city, only chit chatting in spurts. He thought about asking her if something was wrong. Maybe she had a bad day and would rather do this some other time.

Like she had anticipated his question, she spoke up. "I'm so happy we're getting out. Man, it feels like forever since I've been out of town."

Maybe she was just nervous. He felt that way lately, like they were moving on to the next stage of their relationship. "Well, I think Gateway City is great so far. Of course, I haven't lived there as long as you have."

"The town likes you a lot too," she replied.

That statement was a tad odd to him. "The town huh? Well anyone in particular that really likes me?" he chided her.

Samantha replied in a kind of dream like voice, like she had drifted off somewhere outside the car. "My uncle for one. Have I formally introduced you yet? I know you've run into him in town. There's Mr. Tanner, of course. Mrs. Bearstein must tell me every time she comes in to get groceries how great a young man you are."

Justin released a nervous laugh. "Okay. That's all well and good. Is there anyone else that really, really likes me? Because I can only think of one person I feel that way about."

She jerked her as if waking and turned to him. "Oh yeah, right? I really, really like you Justin." She gave a titter, then went back to staring out the window.

"Hey, hon. You sure you're alright? If you got something on your mind, we can still turn around and call this a night."

She turned back to him again and put a hand on his knee. His leg suddenly felt warm. She smiled, more like herself. "I'm sure. Besides, I'm starving."

Dinner turned out to be a lovely affair and Samantha's weird mood dissipated as the night went on. Only when they got back into the car to leave did Samantha veer again into some very strange talk.

"Justin, do we have to go home?"

"I wish we didn't," he said, turning from the road for a split second to give her a goofy wink. "But alas, we have responsibilities to go to in the morn."

"Why would you stay in Gateway City?" she shot back, like she didn't get the joke.

"I like the very relaxed vibe. You're born and raised there, you know. Don't tell me you're getting the big city blues because let me tell you, you have it better where you live."

Samantha sounded grim. "No, but I have craved a change of pace. There are plenty of small towns across America. I know it sounds crazy but, what if we moved to one of those, together."

Justin felt his brain seize up. He couldn't believe what she'd just thrown out. "Whoa, that's a big step. Shouldn't we like, I don't know, go on vacation together first? After the school year, let's plan something."

She blew out a big breath. "Sorry." She let out a nervous laugh. "I hope I didn't scare you off with my crazy idea. It's just that...I really like you, Justin. I want to continue liking you."

Justin couldn't put together what the town and their relationship had to do with each other, but his heart hammered at her comment. All other thoughts were now driven out by the happiness he felt. He reached over with one hand, felt around for hers, and once he had it he squeezed.

Back at his place after dropping Samantha off, Justin rattled around in his bedroom. He couldn't believe the leap they had just taken. He more than liked her, he was pretty sure he had fallen in love with her. The word almost slipped out at dinner.
It had taken all of his willpower not to take her up on her offer to stay the night with her. That would have led to a very tired day tomorrow, which he didn't want to deal with. It was a close call though.
The overhead lights flickered, along with the lamp beside his bed. It went on for what he thought was a strange amount of time. He looked out his bedroom window, he wondered if the wind had picked up or something.
Standing there across the street, looking over to his house, was his bathrobe friend. The man's robe didn't flap and his crazy bed hair ringing his head didn't move. Still, his lights flickered.
"What the hell?" He backed off from the window, feeling creeped out. What was that man doing out there? That's when he realized he didn't even know

the dude's name and couldn't remember ever seeing him around town.

Justin went downstairs to the entryway closet to get the flashlight. He tested it then clicked if off. The lights were still jittering as he walked into the kitchen. He looked out the back door window. A foggy mist seemed to have rolled in since getting home. It stood like a barrier between his house and Samantha's. He didn't understand how that could be causing the flickering. He moved to turn away, when he thought he saw movement in the fog. Something purple. The lights went out completely.

Plunged into darkness, Justin fumbled with the flashlight in his hands. The front door pounded three time, nearly causing him to drop the light. He approached the front on tip toes, as if it might explode inwards. This is crazy. The power just went out, that's all. It's probably Samantha out there because her power went out too.

He left his flashlight off as he approached the door. He looked through the peephole before calling out. The mist was thinner out front. He didn't see anyone standing on his door stoop, but he could swear he saw bathrobe guy still across the street. Now he freaked out.

He was about to snap on his flashlight when the living room flooded with light from outside. He heard the slam of a car door, then pounding again on the door.Instead of heading towards it, he walked backwards towards the kitchen.

Justin kept going until his back knocked into the kitchen sink. He spun around. He could see the mist had increased. It seemed to have a white pearl glow now. It swirled and the little girl came into view. She mouthed something, it looked as if she screamed, her mouth wide, but Justin didn't hear anything. All around his house sat deathly silence. Why couldn't he hear her?

The mist coiled and churned again. Samantha emerged and passed through the girl. Justin blinked and rubbed his eyes. Was he having a dream? Was there ever a little girl? From across the house he heard the pounding of a fist on his front door. This probably wasn't a dream. What was happening, his brain failed to understand.

A rapping came on the back door, gentle in contrast. Justin fumbled to unlock it. He could see Samantha's face set grim in the window as he worked. He opened it a crack and she burst in. With deliberate slowness he shut and locked it.

"Oh, Justin. They started early," she said, low and with a tone of desperate apology. "I think it's because of me."

WELCOME TO COTTONWOOD CREEK

Justin ushered her over to the corner the farthest away from all the windows. He crouched down, his eyes drawn to the mist every few seconds. Samantha joined him.

"What the hell is going on, Samantha? Why is someone pounding on my door like they're the police? Why does it seem like the only house without power is mine? What is the deal with this foggy mist and the little girl? What do you sound so sorry about?"

She took his cheeks into her hands. "Because I like you, I truly do. I should have pushed harder for us to go away. I thought we would be safe but they knew." She let out a bitter laugh. "After all these years I could I delude myself. It always knows."

Justin knocked her hands down. He stood up, indignation filling him. "Are you nuts? Is this some kind of small town prank? Let's mess with the new guy, we got nothing else to do out here."

During the entire conversation the pounding on the door continued. Filled with anger, Justin turned. He planned to stomp across the house and give whoever it was some angry words.

"No." Samantha sounded hysterical. "Don't open the front door. It will come." She grabbed his arm.

"Just what are you talking about?" He turned his anger on her. "What is it?"

Her eyes turned downcast, but not before Justin saw the hurt in them. Instantly he hated himself for attacking her. "I can't tell you. You won't believe me. Just come with me, out the back door. We may be able to get away."

Justin shook off her hand. "I don't believe any of this. I'm not angry at you now. If I find out you are a part of this...I can't say I won't be. This is some messed up stuff. What is this, like a hazing for the new guy in town?"

The knocking stopped and a voice boomed through the door. "Justin, I know you're in there. I need to talk to you."

"Mr. Tanner is the leader of this?" Justin asked. To him the man didn't seem the joking type. He tore open the front door, ready to give him a withering stare before starting in on him.

What greeted him instead, what towered at his front door wasn't a man. A monstrosity stood on his front porch.

The thing towered over him, seven or eight feet at least. Its skin was a gray that made Justin think of rotting flesh that sat at the bottom of a boggy swamp for days. It had no hair, wore no clothes. Its face sagged, its eyes were two huge black holes, sucking all breath from him. The only part they stood out, that seemed defined, were the tiny rows of razor sharp teeth that broke through the skin around its mouth. Behind the thing stood Mr. Tanner, as if he'd brought over a casserole to welcome the new neighbor to town.

"Come out, Justin," Mr. Tanner called.

Even though he felt rooted to the spot, frozen in fear in fact, his body seemed to have a mind of its own and stepped on to the porch.

The creature took a step back as well. With one arm, which ended in four finger hands, which ended at claws that looked like rotten black branches, it pointed to the lawn. Without thought Justin walked to that spot. His mind screamed to run but his body ignored its desperate pleas.

Samantha rushed out of the house. She came to a stop between Justin and the thing. Mercifully, her body partly blocked his view.

"No, Aaron. Can we find someone else? I think Justin can become a part of our community."

Mr. Tanner stepped up to Samantha and put an arm on each shoulder. "I know you went to far, Samantha. We can't have feelings for our food and you know we can't wait. Justin, he's juicy with fear and anger, full of emotion. The Murlak is hungry, it's the spring equinox. Last time, the girl, she wasn't even a morsel even if she hadn't died before he could fully feat." Aaron gave her a hard shove towards bathrobe man. "You don't want to end up like Dennis, do you? You don't want to be the next one to start growing old again?"

Samantha crashed into Dennis, who went down hard on his side. The creature Aaron called the Murlak made a sound, one Justin couldn't even describe. Samantha looked at him, her cheeks wet. She mouthed the words, I love you, and then his sight became blocked as the Murlak reached one slimy, black tree trunk like arm towards him.

That summer a sign went up in the lawn of Justin's house, one that read for sale, call Hometown Homes for details. And on the internet a posting went up, a job opening for a new teacher in the town of Gateway City.

WELCOME TO COTTONWOOD CREEK

SEVERED ATTACHMENTS

Archie tapped Enter on his keyboard for what had to have been the thousandth time that evening. Another electronic order form popped up on his screen. He sighed, leaned back in his faux leather conference chair, and stared out the small window beside his desk. Faint stars dotted the purplish skyline.

I could be over at Gary's playing some D and D and knocking back a few brews right now, he thought, sighing again.

"Not how you'd imagined your Saturday night, huh?" He rotated his chair and faced the desk perpendicular to his. Though DiMandia's face was obscured by her computer monitor, he smiled sheepishly. "Nope," he said, taking the opportunity to fluff his polo shirt up around his gut to conceal his rolls. He was certain DiMandia knew he was chunky. Hell, they'd shared their cramped little office at least five days a week for half a year. But he wanted to look his best. He'd recently discovered she was available. Still married, but available.

DiMandia's chair rolled out from the side of her desk. She smiled, her lush lips caked in black lipstick and sparkling silver glitter. "Me either. But there's no rest for the wicked retail supply merchandisers, right?"

"Exactly. Gotta keep those pencils and pens in stock. I mean, there's not a fucking Staple's right around the corner from every one of our stores or anything."

DiMandia laughed, then snorted, then covered her mouth and nose and snorted behind her palm. Her black pigtails waggled on the sides of her head, causing strands of her mid-back-length hair to flop against her chest.

Her strange laugh made Archie's desire burn ever brighter. Combined with her conservative goth style and all-around friendliness, it was a wonder she'd separated from her husband. The dude must have been a fool to fuck up that relationship. Especially so early in the game--they'd only been married a few months.

"It's not break time, kids," a voice said from the entryway.

DiMandia rolled back behind her desk as Archie hastily rotated his seat to face his screen, trying to appear as if he'd been working. Fuck. Should've kept on the lookout. Their boss, Jack, had a habit of sneaking up on them unawares, especially during the few twenty-second breaks they took to chat. Jack probably thought they were lazy based on the times he caught them bullshitting, and Archie hated that misperception. Especially since he and DiMandia cranked out more approvals than anyone else in the building.

Jack's hollow laugh was full of amusement. "I'm just fuckin' with ya." He stepped up beside DiMandia's desk, a white coffee cup clutched in his right hand.

Mmmm, yeah, Archie thought, stifling a chortle. Jack often reminded him of that boss from Office Space, though he was heavier, completely bald, and had a brown goatee streaked with long white hairs.

"Actually came over to tell you we cut everyone else out already. Fact, I'm 'bout to cut out myself. Got a movie lined up with the girlfriend tonight. Not that it matters much. I'm ready to cut her out too." He chuckled and nodded at DiMandia. "Whaddaya got left there, Mandi?"

"Thirty."

"And you, Arch?" Archie squinted at his screen. "Thirteen."

Jack waved his free hand in a dismissive gesture. "Hell, that can wait 'til Monday. Why don't you two get outta here too, all right?" He made for the door, then wheeled around again. "Oh, and do ya mind walking Mandi out to her car, Arch? Not sure if you've heard about that crazy shit that went on downtown last week, but I don't wanna take any chances. 'Specially with Carl out on hiatus."

DiMandia stood from her desk and stretched. Her knee-high black skirt crept up her light brown thighs, exposing the tops of the black stockings which hugged her legs. "I haven't heard anything."

"Aw, man, it's been all over social media the past few nights. Some jackass is runnin' around robbing people in parking garages. Not your typical muggings, though. They're supposedly hiding beneath cars and slicin' people's ankles with knives or razor blades or something. Crazy, crazy shit," Jack said, shaking his head. "Anyway, you mind doin' that, Arch?"

Archie closed the last open window on his screen and nodded. "Sure thing, boss."

"All right." Silence enveloped the room, and then Jack raised his cup in a mock toast. "Well, you two have a good weekend."

"You too," Archie and DiMandia replied in unison.

Jack left as Archie shut down his computer.

"That's so nineteen-fifties of him," DiMandia said, rolling her eyes. "I'm a grown-ass woman. I can handle myself."

Archie shrugged. "I think it's the gentlemen thing to do. Besides, there aren't any cameras and Carl hasn't been in for a week."

"Good. He gives me the fucking creeps. I wouldn't mind if he never came back."

Archie conceded a nod. The building complex's sole guard was definitely a strange fellow. However, he enjoyed the added benefit of security, and Carl was a decent guy once you got past the stifling aromas of tooth decay and vodka.

"You don't think it's true, do you?" DiMandia asked, slipping her Hello Kitty hoodie on over her blouse. "What Jack said?" "Nah. Just an urban legend. I mean, people are scared shitless to even say 'Merry Christmas' these days. No one is willing to face prison time for a little cash anymore. Not unless they're total Jacks."

DiMandia laughed and snorted again. Archie beamed, pleased she'd remembered his inside term for crazy people. He stood and grabbed his own jacket. "Either way, I don't mind walking you to your car. Just in case."

"I'm sure you don't," she said, and Archie didn't miss the flirtatious edge her voice took on.

He blushed but maintained his composure. Maybe she'd been catching on to his not-so-subtle advances? Not that he cared. He liked her and had kept their relationship professional for the past six months. Now that she was kind of single again, it didn't hurt to show her good men still existed in the world.

Even if she was way out of his league.

DiMandia rushed to the door and flicked the lights off. Then she sped into the hallway and closed the door behind her.

"Hey!" Archie shouted, fumbling around her desk in the darkness. Perspiration coated his armpits instantaneously. *I should've never told her I'm afraid of the dark. She'll never let me live that down.* He stubbed his toe as a light giggle sounded from the other side of the door. He cursed, then crept forward, arms out to ward off any other objects unlucky enough to get in his way.

Seconds later, he wrenched the door open and stepped into the hallway. It was void of life and sound. He shook his head, pulled the door closed, and trekked toward the elevator, certain DiMandia awaited him there.

A figure burst out from behind an adjacent corner and jumped at him.

"Whoa!" he exclaimed. His arms instinctively grabbed at the figure's waist, attempting to keep it at bay.

In the darkened hallway, he and DiMandia stared at each other. Embarrassed, he released his hold on her hips and gulped.

DiMandia batted her eyelashes and giggled anew. "I think someone's a little spooked."

"Well, you are kinda scary."

"I try."

They walked to the elevators side by side, throwing innocent verbal jabs at each other and laughing the entire way. On the ride down to the parking garage, DiMandia inquired about his weekend plans. He didn't know if it was simple idle chit-chat or if she was genuinely interested, but he wasn't going to lie to her. She had spoken of how her husband had lied all the time, and, again, Archie wanted her to know honest men existed. He divulged that he had a hot date with many many-sided dice and some overweight geeks, to which she responded with her signature giggle-snort.

"Now that you know about my exciting plans, how about yours?"

Meh." She shrugged, nonchalant. "Another weekend of wiping my grandma's ass and chasing her damn cats away. The usual."

"Oh, yeah. How's that been working out, by the way?"

"About as well as it sounds."

"It could be worse. I could make you spend a weekend with me and my buddies."

DiMandia raised her eyebrows and pursed her lips. "Yeah. I think I'll stick to the Depends."

The elevator doors opened. Archie stepped out first, tense, the smile melting from his face. The soundless garage was basked in dull yellow light. It stank of piss and dirt, as it had since he'd landed the job a year ago. The new scent--like sloughing, rotting carcass--which had cropped up over the past few days was also present, though dulled.

Really wish they'd let us park on the other side, at street level, like I asked them a few months ago, he thought, glancing all around. Shadows stretched from every nook and cranny like giant black tentacles, damn near swallowing the scant light.

Unexpectedly, DiMandia's hand clenched around his own.

He glanced back and offered a sly grin. "Who's spooked now?"

"Whatevs." She huddled closer as they walked toward her early-2000s rusty Cavalier. "This is for your protection."

Archie didn't argue. He reeled her in closer until her breasts rubbed against his elbow, eyes scanning the garage, ears alert. Her car set alone on the northern end, taking on a brown tinge from the crappy lighting. As they neared it, he released his death-grip on her hand and squatted down to peer beneath the chassis.

"Anything?"

He shook his head and stood back up. "Nada."

"That was easy." She fumbled around in her hoodie jacket and pulled out her keys. Their tinny metallic tinkling echoed tenfold inside the cement garage. "Want a ride to your car?"

Archie glanced over his shoulder, unable to see his car behind the elevator annex. "Nah. Jack's story was obviously bullshit. Besides, I'm a grown-ass man. I can take care of myself," he said in a mocking tone.

She swatted at his shoulder, stepped around him, and reached for the door handle.

Speak, fool! Do what you've been wanting to do for the past few weeks. "Hey, DiMandia. I was, uh, wondering if--"

She wheeled around almost too fast, one eyebrow raised. "Yeah?"

"Well, I know you've been trying to cut ties with your husband and all, and--"

Her hearty guffaw clipped his words off. "Trying? Achilles, dear, I caught him banging my sister in our bed. I didn't just cut ties. I severed that attachment like I was slicing through a hot ham."

Emboldened by her use of his full first name, Archie dug deep inside himself and let it out. "You wanna grab a movie or a dinner--or both--sometime?"

"What, like Netflix and chill?"

"N-no, that's not--I--I didn't--" he stammered. "I meant, like, just getting to know you better. Companionship. I mean, I think we have a good connection. A better connection than we used to have. You're fun and sweet and.... I dunno, maybe it'd turn into something more, over time. Hell, it might even turn out like your husband--ex-husband--like a severed attachment, but it's--I feel--worth a shot, you know?"

Her cheeks darkened. An uncomfortable silence ensued as Archie stood there, waiting for her reply.

Finally, she smiled a warm, genuine smile and said, "With smooth moves like that, how can I say no?"

"Really?" DiMandia nodded.

"Want my digits?"

Archie whipped his cell phone out without answering. She recited her number twice, and he repeated it back. He promised to call--not too soon--and then DiMandia stated she needed to get home.

WELCOME TO COTTONWOOD CREEK

She reached for the car door handle and paused. "You know what? Fuck it." She spun around to face him again.

The blissful look on his face melted away. He didn't want to come off as desperate.

"I haven't hung out with anyone in weeks. Why don't you go home, get cleaned up, then go grab a movie--I like raunchy comedies--and a bottle of red wine and head over? That oughta take an hour or so. Grandma and the cats will definitely be asleep by then."

Archie's confidence and anxiety soared, melding together and twisting his innards. Not willing to look like a complete fool, he agreed in one word and then shut his mouth afterward.

She said a shy farewell and hopped in her car. The Cavalier rumbled to life. Archie stood aside, numb and dumbfounded and more excited than he'd been since he'd last bought a full set of metallic dice.

DiMandia reversed her car, then stopped beside him. She rolled her window down and said in a cheery voice, "Oh, and I like my wine cold." Then she offered a little wave, popped the gear selector, and drove off toward the garage exit.

When she was gone, air rushed from Archie's lungs and his head spun. Holy shit. Did I just do that? A loud cackle escaped his lips. Holy shit! I just did that! Wait 'til Gary and the rest of the guys hear about this!

Elated, he turned on the balls of his feet and meandered toward the elevator annex. He felt crazy and ecstatic for finally working up the nerve to ask her out. The dull yellow lighting and inky stretching shadows soon overtook his happiness, however. As he neared the elevator annex, wetness soaked through his shirt beneath his arms again.

Calm down, dude. You just got a hot date and didn't break a sweat. Don't let a little darkness reduce you to a quivering wuss.

He slowed his pace, took a deep breath, and located his Accord, which was about fifty feet away and enveloped in deep shadow. He stepped away from the quaint yet stench-ridden annex and reached in his right front pants pocket to withdraw his keys.

Something crashed behind him, near the elevator.

He turned, eyes darting, breath escaping in sharp bursts. He withdrew his hand and gripped his house key between his thumb and forefinger, ready to stab away if approached.

A furry little creature hopped off a metallic garbage can near the elevator annex. It landed on the displaced lid which had caused the noise, its tiny claws clattering against it. Something long and white--a chicken bone, perhaps--was clenched within its jaws. Its beady little eyes shone and its wet nose wriggled. Then, ignoring Archie, it scurried away.

Archie gritted his teeth and mentally berated himself. It was stupid to be on edge. The darkness, the stupid little bullshit story Jack had said before he'd left, being the sole person left inside a four-story complex--his imagination was running away with itself. All that paranoid shit should pale in comparison to the joy of finally having a chance with the woman he'd admired for so long.

He wheeled about, pressed the button to remotely unlock the doors, and stomped toward his car. He forced thoughts of DiMandia to the forefront of his mind, unwilling to let his pathetic fears overwhelm him. After a few steps, his mind wandered into the fantasy realm, conjuring pleasant images of how the night might unfold.

The pit of his stomach sank like it'd been tied to a brick and dropped in the ocean. "Shit," he muttered aloud, his voice hushed and hurried. "I didn't even get her damn address!"

He stopped beside his car and pulled out his cellphone, then rifled through the contacts to find the newly added number. He pressed on her name and his thumb hovered over the green phone symbol. Her old Cavalier probably didn't have Bluetooth capability, and she seemed like the type who wouldn't talk or text and drive. Which was a good thing, in his opinion.

Knowing she'd answer when she could, he shot her a quick text. Then he reached for the car door handle, anxious to get home and shower up.

He pulled the door open and placed his right foot in.

A sharp pain ripped across his left ankle.

Archie cried out. His left leg faltered. He reached out and grabbed the door frame, keeping himself from toppling. His cell phone clattered to the floorboard of his car and his knee crashed against the open door, driving stinging needles of pain deeper into his Achilles tendon.

He looked down over his shoulder and caught a stirring of shadow behind him. Then a thin, corporeal figure clawed its way out from beneath his car. It emerged and got to all fours like a dog, grunting and breathing heavily and even reeking of wet dog.

A light mounted to a nearby structural pole flickered, and Archie's imagination raced, surpassing the speed of his heart. The smell, the crazed expression on its hairy face-- it was a beast. A feral beast. He bit down the agony coursing through his leg and started to lower himself into his Accord.

The figure grumbled unintelligibly behind him. Then Archie felt sharp, jagged fingertips dig into the wound on his ankle.

A mortified yell erupted from his mouth. Unbearable pain paralyzed him. He floundered, smashed his head against the steering wheel, and passed out.

***

Archie became aware before he could open his eyes. As fog clouded his memories, darkness passed overhead, then lightness, then darkness, and so on. A musty, musky scent slapped his senses, strangling him.

He gasped for air and his eyelids flew open of their own accord. He squinted as light bombarded his senses. His tongue stuck to the roof of his mouth and exhaustion caressed every limb. Where am I? he wondered. He realized he was lying down and scrambled to sit up. Pain rippled through his left leg and kept him planted in place. Then he recognized his car's back seat and noticed the rumbling of mechanical life beneath him.

He recalled chatting with DiMandia in the parking garage, and her saying something about a steaming hunk of brown-skinned ham and severed attachments, the sting of a blade, a shadowy figure, fingernails digging into his soft flesh--

Fuck! Jack's story--It was true! Panicked, he tried to scoot upward and howled as sharp, stabbing pangs blasted through his injured ankle.

"Wouldn't move too much if I was you," a deep, scratchy voice stated from the front seat. "And stay down. Don't be tryin' no funny stuff."

Something glinted beneath the driver's right elbow. Archie squinted as the Accord hurtled beneath another overpass, providing an ominous transition from light to dark. The barrel of a gun peeked back at him.

He sucked in a sharp breath and stared at the back of the person's head. The guy was shaggy, unkempt, and had either large chunks of dandruff or healthy, well-fed lice speckled throughout the wild tuft of hair atop his skull. And the stench--it was earthy and sour. Overbearing. As if he'd never showered once in his life and had decided to wallow in corpses hours prior.

Archie swallowed, attempting to unglue his tongue from his palate. He winced, mind still sluggish, body slow and achy. "What--I don't have any money, man."

The driver held up Archie's wallet and waved it around. "I know dat. Don't get my kicks from takin' money anyways."

"But...why not just take my car and leave me then?"

"Ain't no fun in dat."

Archie couldn't deny a giggle. "No money, no car? Some mugger you are."

"I ain't no petty mugger, but if dat's what the po-pos think, then I won't tell 'em otherwise." The driver clutched at something on the passenger seat, then brought a clear bottle with red designs on it to his lips. He tilted the bottle and chugged from it.

"Shouldn't drink and drive."

"Dat never stopped your ol' guard, did it?"

Archie furrowed his brow. His mind--and the world around him--whirled. "Carl?"

The man guffawed. "If dat's what you called him, sure. He ain't 'round no more or I'd ask him." He took another quick swig, smacked his lips, and sighed with pleasure. "Last weekend, dat sumbitch caught me crawling 'neath dat ol' Cavalier what's always in ya'lls garage. Had no choice but to beat him down and take all his shit. Had bottles and bottles in his car, dat guy." He chuckled, twisted the lid back onto the bottle, and tossed it aside. "Weren't enough of him left to salvage when I was done with him. Chubby bastard barely fit into the trash can too. S'prised no one found dat body yet. Could smell it a mile away."

Archie's eyes widened. The aroma of death which had invaded the parking garage--that was Carl?

Carl was dead?

He recalled the rat he'd seen, the white thing sticking out of its mouth. I thought it was a scrap, but it must've been . . . Nausea washed over him.

Just then, the message notification for his cell phone sounded. Archie jumped in excitement and patted at his pants pockets, anxious to get the phone out. He'd utter even one word into the receiver if he could, before the crazy mugger shot him.

An icy dread clutched at his throat when he couldn't find the telltale lump, though. Then he remembered he'd dropped the phone to his floorboard during the attack. Helpless and resigned to his captivity, he stared at the barrel still trained on him.

The driver reached across to the front passenger seat. A blue hue lit up the interior of the Accord as he held the cell phone out at arm's length, no hand on the steering wheel. "Well, well, well, lookie here. A message. From some Dee-man-dyuh."

WELCOME TO COTTONWOOD CREEK

DiMandia. Shit. He'd forgotten he'd texted her before the assault. Archie fought back a wave of anxiety and wondered if he'd dragged her into this mess unintentionally. Then wooziness and disorientation and an uncomfortable coldness overtook him. He giggled quietly. I'm fuckin' losing it, he thought.

Pain emanated up from his left ankle, sharp and angry. He glanced at his injured leg as they passed beneath a streetlamp. His foot was bent upward at an awkward angle. A dark, smeared stain stretched from his pant leg to the front of the seat. It was thick and wet, and Archie then understood the source of his sudden, strange hysteria.

"Looks like an address," the driver said, his words garbled and far away. He tossed the phone back onto the passenger seat. "Hot date?"

"Shoulda been, yeah. You kinda fucked that up though, huh?"

"Well, I thought chu was a lady, so you done fucked up my plans, too."

Archie fought to control the gleeful giggles bubbling within his belly. "Why would me having a cock put a damper on your plans?"

"Good point. One holes, two holes--dat don't matter to me, I guess."

Archie's eyelids fluttered and the man's words sank in. A chill drilled into his core, though he wasn't certain if the rampant blood loss was finally catching up or if the realization scared him that much.

He managed to snarl and turned his face in the general direction of the driver, though he couldn't see a damn thing but utter darkness. His voice passed out of his lips in a cool, quiet rush. "I'll bleed out before you even get a chance, you sick fuck."

"Dat's the point, actually." The man spoke over his shoulder, his scratchy voice dripping with menace. "I like 'em cold."

Just like DiMandia likes her wine, Archie mused. He tried to recall more of their warm conversation, but his memories swirled in a cold, grayish haze.

The Accord passed beneath another overpass, and Archie's world darkened forever.

WELCOME TO COTTONWOOD CREEK

DO YOU KNOW THE MUFFIN MAN?

The alarm clock shrieked to life like it did every weekday at 5:08 a.m. Not that Travis needed it too, he never slept good these days. Between the tension of him and his wife working opposite schedules and the phase their three year old son Evan was going through, it was rough.

The past few days his son refused to sleep in his own room, because he was too scared to. Scared of what? Not the dark, or the closet or anything under his bed, he was scared of The Muffin Man. Yes The Muffin Man.

Travis tried not to let it show, how much it frustrated him. His son was scared of a fairy tale, of all things. For whatever reason it may be and it didn't matter the circumstance. Evan do you need to use the potty? No! The Muffin Man will get me! Evan are you ready to go to daycare and see your friends? It's dark outside daddy, I don't want The Muffin Man to get me.

A lot of it, he was sure, were all the changes lately. They had moved into a new home. Evan wasn't the baby anymore in the family, as others had babies that drew attention away from him at gatherings. Most of all though it was the new job his mom had started. Things had changed from her being home every night, helping to tuck him in and partake in bath nights. She had taken a nursing job in a town about an hour away. To make her shift on time, she would leave home by five in the evening and usually wouldn't return until between seven and eight in the morning.

It was hard on Evan, the adjustment to his mommy being gone so much. Travis thought it was even harder on him, but he feigned being supportive to his wife and at the same time feign that everything was cool when it came to taking care of Evan.

He didn't even miss playing video games like he thought he would. He did find himself torn about watching movies, not knowing if he should watch them without his wife or not. Most nights that were not bath night you would find Travis and Evan building race tracks on the floor, playing smash daddy's fingers with his favorite superhero action figures or simply chilling on the couch watching the same cartoons over and over. Cartoons, typical kid stuff, but never anything referencing The Muffin Man, not one time.

This Muffin Man Evan was afraid of was ninja like, sometimes he would be in his room, sometimes in the hallway, kitchen or bathtub. The only consistent trait was it always had to do with the dark or a dark place. Travis searched on his smartphone for reasons why toddlers were afraid of the dark, but none of it seemed to make any sense and most articles he found were rubbish. He tried not to antagonize his son more than once. He would joke about the situation with some of his best liked coworkers, but underneath it all he was becoming frayed. It wasn't simply because of his sons phase or irrational fears, but also because he missed his wife. He tried not to let the ire build in his stomach about cooking and cleaning up every night, or doing the bedtime and morning time routines usually by himself.

******

This night was off to an exceptionally, horrible start.

Travis got off early in hopes of sneaking home for some quality time with his wife. Only when he got there, he found her already gone. She had to drive her mom to and from appointment that day, and he had totally forgotten. The fact did little to ease his ever mounting frustration.

That evening at dinner everything was "yucky" to Evan, then the throwing of food to the floor or on the table started. Travis always tried to set a good example and get his son to eat, but most nights lately he caved and made him a peanut butter and jelly sandwich.

The night went smoothly from there on until bedtime rolled around. Then it was the return of dreaded Muffin Man. Evan was adamant tonight, tears and all that his daddy not leave him in his room. Travis did his normal routine of humoring him by checking under the bed, in the closet, behind the curtains, but this time Evan changed his usual reply. Tonight it wasn't don't let the Muffin Man get me, tonight instead was "Daddy don't go, The Muffin Man is going to get you." Feeling tired and unlike battling with his son tonight Travis asked if he should stay in his room tonight. Evan of course agreed, so he crawled into the twin size bed next to him. Evan gave his daddy the biggest smile as he curled up into a ball next to him.

Travis jumped awake surprised to find himself still in his sons bed. He fished his phone out of his pocket and clicked it to life; 5:04 a.m. He had slept better in the undersized bed than in his own.

Slowly he slid out of the bed as Evan tossed and turned, finding a new position to lay in. Satisfied he was still asleep Travis made his way into the bathroom to get ready for work. He was almost

WELCOME TO COTTONWOOD CREEK

finished with his shower when Evan began screaming.

Travis rushed down the hall to him and found his son in tears repeating over and over that The Muffin Man was going to get him. He calmed him down and the two of them went through their morning routines to finish getting ready.

Once it was time to go Evans reluctance returned. "Don't go outside, it's dark, Muffin Man is out there, I'm scared."

Today was worse than normal, usually if Travis offered to carry him, Evan would drop it. Not today. When he tried to pick him up to head to the door Evan fought him, writhing and wriggling all over the place. Once Travis finally got a good hold of him, he picked him up roughly, demanding him to knock it off as he pulled open the front door and flicked the porch light on.

"Evan look, see? There is nothing out there."

Evan looked for a moment, then buried his face back into his dads shoulder. He began squirming again as they rounded the car to the drivers side, Evan again pleading. Travis flat out ignored him this time as he adjusted the straps of the car seat. He clicked the chest clip into place before the pain erupted in his back and through his body. It burned its way down to his core.

He staggered and turned to see a man smiling at him, waving mildly with the blood covered knife in his right hand. Travis wanted to lunge at him, to protect his son but his arms wouldn't move. As he went to step forward the smiling stranger jabbed the knife into his throat and made a sideways motion. Travis felt like he couldn't breathe, like he was drowning as he collapsed to his knees and went face first into the dirt next to the man's beat up brown boots.

    Travis was only aware of two things as he took his final muddled breaths, the sound of his son crying helplessly in his car seat and the sound of the stranger lowly and creepily singing "Do you know the muffin man, the muffin man..."

WELCOME TO COTTONWOOD CREEK

Jany-Jay Does a Duet

"Time for the five o'clock rock out, with my mop out!" Jay said aloud, flicking his tongue whilst raising his fist and making the sign of the horns. "Ooh, yeah!" he continued, mimicking Randy "Macho Man" Savage as he eyed the ladies' toilet door.

With his other cleaning duties done, including the male toilets, this was his last port of call before clocking-off; the women's toilets were always his last job of the day, because it gave pupils/teachers time to leave the school. That way Jay could get on with his work in peace without having giggling girls pestering, asking for fags, flirting with him or making a general nuisance of themselves.

A smile flashed across his face as he slid his mop and bucket across the well-polished floor from the men's to the women's.

Horny sixth form girls are the best, man! he thought, hitting play on his Casio tape deck, his ears filling with Jailhouse Rock.

"Don't ever let them tell you CDs are better, ladies--they're for faggots and soft boys." He'd once told a group of tittering teen girls whilst mopping a hallway floor. "If you see a guy using tapes, you know he's a real man, baby, just like Elvis was."

This prompted Jay to wink at them and run his hand through his quiff whilst thrusting his hips, making the keys on his janitor belt shake, rattle and roll. "Love me tender, ladies!" he'd called after them, pointing and chuckling as the girls tittered and scurried down the corridor like rats up drainpipes.

As the rock 'n' roll pounded around inside his skull, Jay got on his tip-toes, snaked his hips, curled his upper lip and started singing into the haft of the mop handle as though it were a microphone.

"They threw a party in the jail . . ." Jay crooned, spinning on his heel, pressing his back to the door, and easing it open with the flat of his foot. ". . . The prison band began to wail . . ." Grabbing his balls, gently, he did a Michael Jackson jiggle of them and entered the toilets.

"Sweet. Fuck!"

He removed his headset and placed it around his neck, The King now singing to the veins and Adam's apple in Jay's throat, and looked at the mess before him. He spotted chewing gum stuck to the partitions, lipstick on the mirrors, toilet paper strewn across the floor, puddles of water, wrappers, empty cigarette boxes, cans and bottles, used tampons, blood up bins, snot down walls, graffiti . . .

WELCOME TO COTTONWOOD CREEK

"What is that smell? Has a fucking rat scurried up a piss-soaked cunt and died?" He slid his bucket inside and went back to his trolley to gather a few things he'd need: sweeping brush, black bag, various sprays, rags, and a dustpan. "Goin' to take me a fucking hour to sort that shithole out, man. Will ol' Jany-Jay here get extra? A slice of overtime pay? Will Jany-Jay fuck. Frugal fucks."

Sighing, Jay put his work tools down on the shelf above the sinks, brushing debris off it and onto the floor, and then grabbed his brush in readiness to sweep the floor. As he walked back towards the door, a piece of wall art grabbed his attention, making him grin.

The graffiti depicted a huge bleeding heart with an arrow slammed through it, complete with feathers and names etched inside the cartoon-sized organ.

"Janice luurvs Janitor JayMan and his shafty mop head! XXXX!!!" he read aloud.

Wet little bitches.

"Go on, show us your dick!" one of Janice's friends had asked him one afternoon, a few weeks back, when he'd gone in to clean. He'd caught them smoking and talking about boys.

"Maybe I will, if I can nick a smoke?"

"Shit, you won't tell on us will you, Jay?" one of the other girls asked, biting her nails and looking at her friends. "Mum will ground my arse 'til doomsday."

Always a fat one in the bunch.

"Depends if I get that fag or not, Jennifer."

"Uh-huh, the cig is for a glimpse of your sausage!" Carla smirked.

Jay smiled, "I think that'd be going too far, ladies. Watch this." Jay grabbed his mop, threw his head back, and placed the tip of the handle on his chin so that the whole thing was pointing towards the ceiling. He then snaked his hips as he balanced the cleaning implement.

The girls laughed, clapped, and encouraged him to sing as he did his party trick. Once he was done, he placed the mop to one side and started juggling bottles of cleaning fluid.

Carla screeched, "I bet you got all the moves in the sack, too."

Janice winked. "I wouldn't mind finding that out. Look, his dick is pushing against the front of his trousers!"

Jennifer choked on a laugh, and smoke blew out of her nostrils. "He's pretty happy to see us!"

"Right, out you go, ladies--a man has a job to do."

WELCOME TO COTTONWOOD CREEK

    Shaking his head, Jay replaced his headset, looked down at the floor and started to sweep the litter from behind the sinks and bins before moving over to the six cubicles to sweep them out one at a time.

    All the while Elvis continued to pound in his ears. When he came to the third cubicle door, he noticed it was locked.

    "Goddamn it! Not again." Jay rapped his knuckles against his legs. "They only do it to wind me up. Bitches."

    He went back to the second cubicle, stood on the pan, and peered over the top of the partition to see down into the toilet with the locked door.

    One of these days, I'm going to see one of them pissing, their knickers around their ankles. A smile pulled across his lips. By using the handle of his brush, he nudged the lock on the door to disengage it.

    "Ugh!" he huffed, stepping in front of the door that had been locked.

    With the third swept down, he moved on to do the fourth and then fifth. When he came to the final door, it too was locked from the inside.

    "Girls, girls, girls . . . You really are asking for a spanking--" he thought he heard someone giggling from in there. "Hello?" he tapped on the door.

"Housekeeping!" His smile widened. "I have some fresh towels for you. Would you like me to turn down your bed?"

Now, if there is a girl on the loo, Jay thought, I might get in trouble, but then he relaxed. He knew most of the children and they loved him. They wouldn't grass on him for being a little strange. Besides, he wasn't doing anything wrong. It wasn't like he was spying or wanking. Jay knew where to toe the line. Flirting's harmless. He'd never pinched a bum, wolf-whistled, or done anything else along those lines. He kept his hands to himself.

Jay tapped on the door again. Got to be empty. I've never, ever seen a girl in here after school hours. Not in all the years I've been doing this job.

Don't Cry Daddy started playing on his Casio-- the song had driven tears from him the very first time he'd heard it at his grandfather's funeral, almost fifteen years ago. Jay had been close to the man, who had been like a second father to him, and Jay had gained the love of Elvis from him.

"One of these days, I swear! I'll ring the little shits' necks. Bet you anything it's Janice who does this." He couldn't help but smile as he made his way into cubicle five to step on the pan to get his brush over the top of the partition to unlock the door.

WELCOME TO COTTONWOOD CREEK

Huh, maybe I'll find . . . His thoughts trailed off, his mouth swung open, and his eyes bugged . . . Elvis . . . Sat on the toilet was Mr. Higgins, the gym instructor. His face ashen, his lips a blue/purple--in his left hand he clutched a pair of pink knickers, in the other, his small floppy cock. A fart squeaked from the cadaver. Shock was replaced by amusement, and Jay started howling with laughter.

"Tut, tut, Mr. Higgins! What will Mrs. Higgins think? Well, she'll find out after I report this mess."

By using his brush, Jay repeated his trick and disengaged the lock. After stepping down from the toilet, he went to the main door and locked it with his keys.

Let's have a bit of fun first . . . After all it's not every day I find Elvis dead on the porcelain!

"How about a duet, Mr. Higgins?"

Jay moved to the last door on the left, opened it inch by inch with a creak punctuating every move and stared at the body when it was in plain view.

Into the Ghetto replaced Don't Cry Daddy and Jay stopped the tape.

"You can be my Lisa Marie on this one, Donald," he said, going to the gym teacher and giving his limp leg a kick. A fresh laugh tore through Jay when he saw the man's green shorts and pants that had been thrown to one side. "Must have been eager to pump one out, big fella? I wonder if I can lug you around..."

Jay knew he'd be able to pick the bigger man up, as he was no slouch at six-two and two-hundred-twenty-two pounds. Before grabbing Donald and hoisting him up off the bog, Jay looked at the knickers and spied a name etched on the waistband.

"Priscilla. Priscilla Latch? The girls' gym teacher? You dirty fuck, Donald--she must be half your age. More, maybe!"

Thinking the whole thing will be embarrassing for the man's wife and his colleagues here at Pont-Y-Porth High School for girls, Jay couldn't help but laugh once more as he grabbed Donald and hugged him close to his chest.

"Are you ready, Don? We're going to have a wee dance and sing-song, son,." Jay said, turning the man's head so he could look into Donald's dead white eyes.

A teeth-chattering chill seeped off Donald and found its way under Jay's clothes, but it didn't stop him from hitting play on his tape deck.

"Here we go. When I stop singing that'll be your queue to start. Got it? Also, try and put on your best Marie voice, son."

A surge of excitement coursed through Jay as he danced the body out into the toilet's main area and swept it around and around in circles as he sung his heart out. All the while the dead man's head bobbed and flopped on its fat plinth with its toes dragging along the tiles.

"Your turn!" Donald didn't sing, so Jay stopped moving and drew the headset off his head. "What's the matter? Frostbite? Rigor mortis got your mouth clamped shut? Some fucking fun you--"

"Kiss me, fat boy!" Donald yelled, his head slumping forward, issuing a snapping sound like a hundred icicles breaking at once.

Jay screamed, feeling hot piss shower down his left leg. "You . . . you're . . ."

"Dead?! Ha!" When Donald spoke, thick fog emanated from his mouth and nostrils--the temperature in the room plummeted. Jay shrieked when he saw the sinks, taps, pipes and floor cover with thick ice. The room resembled a meat locker.

"This . . . can't . . . Ugh!" he wheezed. The cold caught in his throat, squeezing his windpipe to the size of a pinprick. Jay felt his body begin to freeze--ice climbed his legs and found its way into his ball bag, hips, and guts. His organs grew frosty and laden--his heart slowed to a death-pace.

More pain exploded in his lower back as Donald's grip intensified, his nails digging into Jay's flesh. Jay grew an icicle-beard within seconds, and heard his bones start to splinter like window panes.

"Lights out, Hound Dog!" Donald said.

"N--n--no--" Jay managed, his teeth clinking together and crumbling to frost particles. The last thing Jay heard was his spine break and his ribcage collapse.

WELCOME TO COTTONWOOD CREEK

The Vessel

I woke up feeling like my head had been sawn in half. The pain was excruciating. It took every effort to open my heavy eyes enough to see. I was definitely not home in my poky one-bedroom flat in the middle of Durham. Strong feelings of panic and fear filled me. Terror threatened to take over.

With difficulty, I began to take in my surroundings. I was in a square room with a concrete ceiling and something like padding covered the walls. The only light was coming from a dim bulb hanging alone above me. I looked around for a window or door and in abject horror realised the room was made of solid materials, no entry or exit anywhere. How is that even possible?

Something was really wrong. My legs wouldn't move, not one single inch. They felt like lead. I didn't want to look. I felt shocked at the thought that my legs may no longer be there. My bladder released warm urine and I felt it pooling underneath me. Shame, mixed in with everything else threatened to overwhelm me.

I had to know. Taking a deep breath, hesitantly I glanced down. My legs were indeed still there but my thighs, knees, calves and ankles were strapped down with thick leather straps. I was on some sort of old dentist chair angled so that I was lying partly upright. Fear like I had never known overtook me. I couldn't hold back the flood of salty tears streaming down my face and reaching my dry, parched lips. Through my sobs I heard a whimper, like an animal that was injured and in pain. I thought I was hearing things until I heard it again, louder this time.

Was there an animal in here with me? Why did I not see it before, or hear it? I shivered involuntarily, inhaled a deep breath and turned my head at a painful angle towards where I thought the pitiful sound was coming from. A bright flash hurt my eyes and through the dancing coloured spots I gasped as a bright spotlight shone into a corner of the room. It garishly shone on what I had been unable to see in the dim light. I wished my eyes had never opened.

In a solid steel cage was a young girl, huddled in one corner in what looked like a flimsy nightgown. Shivering and crouched down, it was as if she was trying to not be seen, hiding in the shadows that didn't exist. She was filthy dirty with greasy long hair partly hiding her face. Her arms, hands and feet were black with something dark. Suddenly she flinched and I saw an eye glinting, looking right at me. She howled. It was a deep, guttural, animalistic harrowing noise.

WELCOME TO COTTONWOOD CREEK

"Shh. It's okay" I whispered. "I won't hurt you. What's your name?"

With a voice barely audible, she responded "Vessel, I am Vessel".

What kind of name is that? It chilled me, nothing made sense and it dawned on me she'd been here for a lot longer than me. Why was she caged while I was restrained? Both trapped in this godforsaken place together.

"Vessel, how long have you been in here? Do you know?"

There was no answer, just empty silence. The girl turned her head away, hugging her knees and rocking back and forth humming a tune I could not recognise to herself.

Harsh, blinding fluorescent lights came on overhead, hurting my eyes. The entire room was now completely exposed and revealed. I now really knew what Hell looked like: this room with no doors or windows. I was alone with Vessel.

I felt like I was losing my sanity, giggling ridiculously to myself as I thought You are not in Kansas anymore Dorothy!

A deep voice boomed and vibrated through the air.

"Let the giving and taking begin"

It sounded like it came over a speaker system. I frantically looked for where it might be placed. There was someone else. We were not alone. Hope surged through me.

"Help! Please help, we are in here!" I yelled.

My cries were met with a long heavy silence.

It was then that I felt a sharp pain in my left arm and looked down instinctively. A cannula was placed deep in my forearm with a single, thick tube trailing from it. I had no idea how I had not noticed this before. Frantically I went to pull it out of my arm, only to realise in defeat that my upper arms were strapped tightly to the chair. I was not going anywhere. A scream erupted from me as anger and fear took over. I stared in absolute horror at my blood travelling down the tube at a pace I didn't think was possible.

The girl was agitated by now and hysterical laughter burst from her mouth. She pointed at me then at herself. "Me Vessel! Me Vessel".

Feeling like I was going to vomit, I followed the tube with my eyes and watched the other end dripping dark, visceral, thick blood. My precious blood. The rapid drops filling a metal bowl fixed at mouth level to the cage. She looked at me, grinning manically before plunging her face towards the bowl, I could hear her lapping hungrily like a wild animal.

My life blood continued to fill the bowl. The constant rapid drops were now the sound of certain death.

I felt I was going to completely lose my mind – I had to turn away. I just couldn't. I was fixated on the girl continuing to slurp my blood from the bowl. She clapped her hands in glee, bouncing on her haunches, just like a child that had been given a new toy.

As I began to slip into unconsciousness, she glared at me, dark, thick blood dripping from her chin, her teeth stained pink as she grinned at me. There was no resemblance to a girl anymore. Through a haze I heard her voice.

"Me Vessel"

Our eyes stayed locked together as I faded away into an empty black place.

The Vessel, sated after her fill, curled up and waited to meet the next Giver.

The giving and taking, for now, was complete.

THE END

WELCOME TO COTTONWOOD CREEK

Pure Schitt Luck

So if you found this letter, I'm already gone. I mean, not like dead or anything, just not here anymore. Hopefully not dead anyways.

I've been leaving my story at record stores for a while now. Each time I write it I think I say it better. Or maybe remember it less. Either way, when I write it down, the horror of it all seems to become third person, like it happened to someone else, and I feel a bit more relief.

The ritual is the same. I find a record store, I secure said store against the shamblers, and I write my story by candlelight while I listen to music on this old mp3 player. I'll hang around for a few days, scavenge supplies, and look for a laptop with some juice left so I can rip more music onto the player. Then I travel on to look for the next shop.

So, if you're reading this, I'm gone. Have a drink and a story.

The night before the world went to shit, I was drunk. I mean, I was really drunk. I woke up in the closet at this house party. It was a nice roomy closet, but a closet nonetheless. It had sliding doors, and a shirt was wedged between the door and the jamb.

That little opening let in enough bright eye-stabbing sunlight into my closet to wake me up.

Soft moaning came from just outside my door. I sat there for a minute rubbing my temples to the beat of my pounding head trying to figure out what was up. I was pretty sure people were making out mere feet away from me. I stretched a bit, trying to shake the pins and needles out of my left foot. My fingers pulsed at the tips in the indentations that the bass strings left, and my shoulder hurt. After a bit, I was more than pretty sure people were making out mere feet away from me.

I slowly pulled open the door and crawled out. The light was extra stabby once I was completely out of the closet. After blinking a few times, I looked up at the bed. It was rocking a little, and I saw Danny's boots and a smaller pair of red sneakers dangling over the edge. I was at the same time happy and grossed out; happy that Danny was still here, but grossed out because he was getting all makey outy in the same room as me. I didn't want to hear--or see--any of that.

Standing up as quietly as I could, I went through the slightly open bedroom door into a dark hallway. There were a few people leaning against the wall in various stages of hungover, and they all were waiting in line for the bathroom. Seeing everyone lined up seemed to stir something in my bladder, because all of a sudden, I really had to piss. However, no one seemed to be in any rush, and the current occupant started loudly tossing their cookies in the bathroom, so I figured I'd take my business elsewhere.

The front room was in much the same situation as the hallway. People were strung out all over the furniture and floor. One dude was sitting up as I walked into the room. Blearily he looked at his watch and muttered under his breath. I nodded to him as he turned to the girl on the couch next to him. He shook her, saying something along the lines of "we gotta go to bed," but I was already out the front door before I heard a response.

It was a cool morning, but I could tell it would be hot later. The humidity in the air coated my skin with a sticky film. A light breeze stirred around me, blowing the smell of cigarettes and stale beer off my clothes and hair directly into my face. It made my head hurt worse. I found a tree to duck behind and took a piss.

Just as I was shaking off the Shatner I felt someone touch my shoulder. I jumped a little and swung around to see some dude trying to grab at me. He had weird sores on his face and neck, and he moved with jerky, twisty motions. His jaw kept moving around like he was chewing on one of those really chewy rolls from the lunchroom at my old high school. I backed away and told him to back off, but he wouldn't back up, so I backhanded him.

    He didn't even flinch, and I had hit him hard. He just kept coming at me. I balled up my hand and punched him dead in the nose. His head flopped backwards and he did this slow motion, cartoonish, backwards fall. He tried to keep walking forward, but his head looked like it was staying in the same spot. He kind of crumpled backwards and fell on his back, his jaw still moving. I didn't wait around to see if he was okay. A dude like that coming up to you when you're taking a piss is a clear sign that it's time to leave. I finished zipping up my pants and went back inside to get Danny.

    Here's where we gotta back up a bit. Danny was the vocalist. He could play some guitar too, but we mostly left that up to Stan. I play the bass, and Paul plays the drums. We really needed a second guitarist, but for whatever terrible, terrible reason, Danny got us a keyboardist instead--Chance. With Chance in the band we sounded like one of those Swedish metal bands with too many weird instruments and some chick singing about ships and sailors and shit. Only, we didn't have a hot chick singer--we had Danny.

WELCOME TO COTTONWOOD CREEK

Ugh. Keyboard metal.

Anyways, the night before my closet sleepover, we had played a gig at Schitt Hole. No, really. Schitt Hole. The bar was named after the owner, Travis Schitt. He was a really cool guy, but everybody made fun of his name. They kept calling him Travis Tritt. His Schitt Hole was this dive bar downtown that had been a speakeasy during Prohibition. There was a door with a sliding window and everything. You didn't have to say a password, but you got the feeling you needed to know what it was. You went down this narrow ass staircase into the basement, and the place seemed to be twice as big. The walls were covered in band posters that dated back to the eighties and were held up by stickers and sticky spots from dried beer, blood, and other dubious substances. The ceiling was made of those thick acoustic tiles; most of them were painted black, and most of them were cracked, but a couple of them had been replaced a decade ago without being painted.

The stage was about six inches taller than the rest of the floor, which meant you were six inches closer to the low ceiling. Danny was tall, so when we played there, he usually grabbed the mic and wandered around in the crowd at the front of the stage. We broke a few mic cables that way, but we always drew a big crowd, so we never got charged for them.

There was a second, even narrower stairway that led from the back of the stage and out into the alley. Steve parked his van there in the alley and we loaded gear into the bar that way. That night, as Danny was pulling Steve's cabinet out of the back of the van, this stringy haired hobo jumped out from nowhere, grabbed him, and bit him on the neck. Steve leapt into action and just started throwing jab after jab into the hobo's face, then twirled him around by the shoulders and kicked him in the ass. The hobo belly flopped hard on the concrete, then slowly got up and stumbled off in the other direction. Meanwhile, Danny was coming up with some pretty colorful new lyrics to the song he'd been writing called "Shit I Say When I'm Angry," while Chance and Paul helped him put the cabinet down. I had just come back up from loading in some of the drums.

"Dude, are you okay?" I yelled, running up to Danny.

"That fucking HURT," Danny said, placing angry emphasis on each word.

"Are you bleeding?" I said, grabbing a t-shirt out of the merch tote.

WELCOME TO COTTONWOOD CREEK

Danny pulled his hand off of his neck. There was a little rivulet of blood dripping from a small puncture surrounded by teeth marks.

"Shit," I said, trying to dab at it with the t-shirt.

"Fuck off," Danny said, slapping the shirt away.

"Dude," that looks fuckin badass!" Chance said, his hands on his hips. "You should let the blood dry. It'll look awesome!"

He had this look on his face like a kid seeing a snake eat a rat in science class, and he nodded his head as he spoke, like some sort of douchey bobblehead.

Fucking keyboard players.

"Whatever," Danny said. "Let's get the gear in."

Danny grabbed Steve's cab roughly and kicked open the back door, all while Steve watched and cringed. Chance grabbed something light and ran after him.

Not much of note happened for a while. Danny cleaned off his neck, much to Chance's chagrin. The first band played, and we all drank beers and such. The second band started setting up, and we drank more beers and such. Then they finished and it was our turn.

You know how I said we drank beers? Well Danny drank more beers than any of us. By the time we took the stage, he was hammered. We blew through our first two songs, then he told the story about how he got bit by a hobo in the alley and how Steve kicked his ass. He then renamed our third song "Hobo Bite Ass Whoopin," and we dove into it.

There is a long instrumental part in that song, and during this part, Danny decided to run through the crowd biting people. Arms, necks, shoulders. He bit this one girl on the ear and she slapped the shit out of him. The crowd loved it.

We finished our set and the manager came up to us with a tray of shots. Steve was the driver, so he declined. Danny was too busy hitting on the chick he had bitten, so he didn't get his. Chance turned his shot down because he's a keyboard player. So I took four of the shots, and Paul took the other one. Let me tell you, nothing sobers you up quicker than four shots in a row after several hours of drinking.

Somehow, Danny, Chance, and I ended up at this house party with a bunch of the people from the bar. We walked in and were met with yelled drunken greetings. Everybody was trying to give us beers and high fives. We felt like rock stars--especially Danny. He jumped up onto the couch and sprayed beer all over everybody. We toasted to a kick ass show, and then I shotgunned a beer. After that, it gets kind of fuzzy. I remember Danny biting more people, and getting into at least one fight. I remember this not so hot, but not so choosy girl that was all over me. I vaguely remember throwing up on her shirt before she stormed off. Then I woke up in a closet.

Now you're caught up.

So after that dude tried to grab me while I was pissing, I was in no mood for anymore antics. I was grumpy and my head hurt. Those shots had felt like a bad idea when I took them; the morning after proved it. I stormed back into the house to go get Danny.

Of all people, the first person I run into is Chance. I expected him to be chipper as hell, because he liked to tell us how he was a morning person, but he looked like he had just seen a ghost.

"Dude, I think that girl died," he said, pointing towards the couch.

The guy that was trying to wake up his girlfriend earlier was pacing back and forth with his hands on his head. The girl who he was trying to wake up was sitting motionless, her head back against the back of the couch. Her eyes were open, and her skin seemed to be the wrong color. Another girl was on her phone, cussing and freaking out.

"They can't get a hold of the police," Chance said. "She called like five times already but keeps getting a busy signal."

"This is fucked up," I said, my flesh crawling. "I gotta get Danny, and we gotta go."

Chance nodded silently in agreement.

Suddenly I felt very, very sober, and very afraid. I tripped over someone in the hallway. I whipped around to yell at the person, but the words caught in my throat. It was one of the dudes in line for the bathroom, and he had collapsed in a pool of vomit. Blood oozed from his nose and mouth. His skin was turning a veiny purple and his open eyes looked wrinkled and bloodshot.

I heard someone inside the bathroom scratching at the door and I panicked. Tripping over the body again, I rushed into the bedroom and found Danny there still on top of the girl.

"Man, you gotta get up, we gotta go," I said, tapping him on the shoulder. "Take her with us."

The whole time I was tapping his shoulder, I was looking at the door. I knew that any minute something fucked up was gonna happen, and I knew it was coming through that door.

But I was wrong.

Danny grabbed my wrist, and his hand was ice cold. I looked down in time to see him open his jaw and crane his neck to bite my wrist. I jerked my arm out of his grasp, horrified as I saw his face. His mouth stayed open; he was missing teeth now, and the ones that were left were bloody and had chunks of flesh and hair stuck in between them. He was wriggling like he was trying to get up, but couldn't quite do it. Strange, terrifying noises issued from his open mouth accompanied by the smell of rotting meat and stale beer.

I backed away and realized that Danny couldn't get up because he was laying on top of the girl from the show, and she was on top of his arm. Her shirt was off, and oozing bite wounds pockmarked her chest. Her pink bra was speckled with crimson splotches, like grotesque polka dots. I tried not to look at her face, but I did it anyways. The skin on one side of her face had been ripped completely off from her cheekbone, down her neck, to the top of her collarbone. Her exposed teeth looked like a gruesome smile, and her open eyes made it worse.

I backed out the room quickly and slammed the door shut behind me. Something grabbed my arm, and I turned. It was a chick in a spaghetti strap shirt and sunglasses. I felt relieved for a moment, but then she lurched forward and her glasses fell off, with one of her eyeballs still attached to a lens. I shoved her down the hall as hard as I could and jumped over the pool of vomit on the floor.

The body that had been there was gone.

I heard more scratching and strangled gurgling noises from the bathroom and thought my heart was gonna burst through my chest. Then someone started screaming in the front room. I rounded the corner to find the dude with the dead girlfriend trying to shove her back off of him. Suddenly she was less dead and trying to bite him. Blood and saliva dripped from her mouth onto his face as he screamed. Several other people were nearby crumpled on the floor, twitching and vomiting.

"Dude, help him!" Chance yelled suddenly, snapping me out of shock.

I kicked the girl hard in the head, dislodging her from the guy. He shoved her off and he ran, stumbling out the door.

"I could use a bit of help too," Chance said, breathing heavily.

I turned around and saw the vomit puddle corpse trying to eat the keyboard player's face. I kicked the dude hard in the side, feeling ribs crack under the sole of my boot. Vomit corpse lost its grip on Chase, who immediately shoved himself free.

"Thanks," Chase said, breathless. "Where's Danny?"

I couldn't speak. I just shook my head.

"Let's get out of here," Chance said, moving towards the front door.

WELCOME TO COTTONWOOD CREEK

I followed, but suddenly dead couch girl grabbed me by the belt and pulled herself up towards my chest. Her pink nails dug into my shirt and she hissed, her taut muscles making her twitch and sway like an old branch in a high wind. I pushed hard on her forehead, but her hand was caught up in my belt and I couldn't dislodge her.

Chance was there in an instant. He grabbed a floor lamp and hit her in the side of the face with the base. He hit her again and again until her neck snapped and her head lolled to the side. Her grip loosened enough on my belt that I was able to wrench free and shove her to the ground.

"Go!" Chance yelled, pointing at the door.

Two dudes had appeared behind him, and he was whacking away at them with his lamp. Chance caught one in the head and knocked him over.

"Take that," Chance yelled, sounding frantic.

"Come on, Chance," I yelled, grabbing him by the back of the jacket.

He stumbled backwards with me, and I pulled him out the door. I jumped off the porch and ran into the yard, but stopped dead when I heard Chance yell. I whipped around to see him on the porch, the cord from the damn floor lamp wrapped around his leg. I rushed to help him, but it was too late. Couch girl and one of the big guys grabbed a hold of Chance by the legs and dragged him back into the house. In the dim light, I saw the girl rip this throat out with her teeth as the big guy tore open his abdomen at the belly button.Chance had probably saved my life, only to die like that. What a shitty way to go.

The next few months drug by for me the same way it had for other survivors. I never found my other band mates; their apartments were abandoned and crawling with face munchers.

I scavenged food and water, found supplies where I could, and avoided zombies like the...well, like something terrible. I never really trusted anyone even before they were trying to eat me, so I traveled alone. As time passed, I felt more and more crazy. It got to the point that I was going on fifteen minutes of sleep at a time, snatched in between hours of constantly watching my back.

Then one day I stumbled across a record store. It was in a brick building downtown in a smallish city I was passing through. No one was inside, nor were there any wandering face eaters nearby. I got in through a broken window in the back. With crates of records everywhere and big heavy shelves, it didn't take long to secure the building. There was a laptop in the back, and on a whim, I fired it up.

It worked, and it had lots of music on it.

WELCOME TO COTTONWOOD CREEK

    I found headphones threw them on, one ear on one ear off, and just listened to music for the first time in months. It was like a salve on my fried nerves. I felt relaxed and awake again. The laptop battery died later that night, but the record store became my home base for the next few days. I dug around and found an mp3 player with a bunch of stuff on it with a solar powered battery charger nearby. Whoever invented the solar battery charger deserves a medal.

    One day I wandered into a liquor store. There on a middle shelf was the same whiskey that Travis Schitt brought me on that tray so many nights ago. I looked at the bottle, smiled, and then threw it across the store. That whiskey was terrible.

    I did, however, find a few bottles of something nicer, and decided I needed a drink. I went back to the record store and had a few shots, listened to my mp3 player, and slept like a fucking baby. When I woke up, I had a clear head for the first time in months. I realized how lucky I had been: had it not been for Travis Schitt bringing me those shots, I wouldn't be here anymore. I would have been sober enough to try my luck with that girl, been turned down, drank even more at the party, and would've ended up dead or one of those flesh eating dick heads roaming the streets.

I also realized how shitty everybody has it now.

Whoever you are, I hope you find a peace of your own. A clear head and a calm mind these days is worth more than a store full of canned food. If you've found this letter, you and I are kindred spirits of sorts. With that in mind, I offer you a drink and a safe place surrounded by music. Within these walls, may you find solace from insanity, and may you catch a good buzz while doing so.

Also, may you never waste your battery life on keyboard metal.

Keyboard metal sucks.

WELCOME TO COTTONWOOD CREEK

NIGHT SCHOOL

"Why am I such a fucking pushover?" The thought was resounding in Tyler's head as he made his rounds through the hallways of the empty school around midnight. He never understood the point of this so called "senior week" nonsense the administrative team made such a big deal out of. They made it seem like a group of covertly trained high school kids were going to break into the building in the middle of the night and rob the place blind. What pissed him off most was even though he and whoever else from his team did their overnight sentence there was a strong chance someone from said administrative team would be in on some kind of senior prank and let them in the school with permission anyways.

Tonight was already off to a bad start, he had forgotten to go pay his cell phone bill earlier that day and now he had no service and the school Wi-Fi network blocked most of what anyone would find entertaining. So he tossed in his earbuds and strutted down one hall after another listening to some old school nineties gangsta' rap. Something about the music mixed with the red glow of the exit signs illuminating at the end of some of the dark hallways made him feel like he was in a movie and hiding from people outside looking for him. He finished making his rounds half ass checking the exit doors to make sure they were indeed locked and made his way to the teacher's lounge for a Mountain Dew and a Honey Bun, that was unless the bitch from the first floor hadn't gotten them all already. He swore whenever he went in there she was already buying the last one, like she knew he wanted that sweet treat and wanted to give him a big fuck you.

He was in luck tonight, the old hag hadn't gotten them all during the day! Tyler punched in the number on the panel and watched his beloved snack cake fall. He made his way back down stairs and to the front of the building where the security office was located. He sat down and propped his feet up on the desk as he devoured his midnight snack and watched the monitors housing the video feeds of the seventy plus security cameras throughout the inside and outside of the school building.

Sitting there watching the cameras at some point

he must've dozed off, he jumped with a startle as he almost fell off of the chair as the wheels kicked back. Tyler hopped to his feet and gained his bearings while laughing at himself. As he stretched and looked at the clock he realized he had been asleep for almost two hours!

"Well shit" he said aloud, "Good thing no one is splitting this shift with me tonight or I'd of been in deep doo doo! But that's what I get for letting them give me two nights in a row of this crap when everyone was supposed to get one night each."

He decided it was time to make another lap around the creepy ass school to wake himself up. Times like now he wished at least there was an overnight custodian or someone to talk to. All his friends had day jobs, so he couldn't of called them even if he had remembered to pay his damn phone bill.

Tyler made his way up the stairs nearest the front doors, stopped to take a piss and made his way down one of the English hallways and into the adjoining Science wing. He was about halfway down the hall when he first heard the moaning type noise. At first, he assumed it was the wind until he heard the definitive sound of someone banging against some lockers from what he was guessing was somewhere beneath him on the first floor.

"Fan-fucking-tastic" Tyler thought to himself as he quickly made his way to the closest stairwell and began his descent. About four steps from the first floor the few lights on in the building flickered and then died making it incredibly dark and hard to see. He reached for his cell phone and popped on the flashlight. He aimed it down the hallway in both directions, it looked clear, nothing but blue lockers lined each wall, with some random half assed school projects tacked up above them.

The shuffling of feet drew his attention back to the left, he swung his light in that direction. He caught a glimpse of someone as they ducked into the doorway of one of the art rooms. They started banging against the door, groaning as if they were in pain. Tyler resisted the urge to call out to them and instead crept closer down the hall. He got within a few feet of the individual when they stopped, as if they could sense his presence behind them. Their breathing picked up as their shoulders started to heave. Tyler fell to his ass when they spun around. It was a student, one with a serious fucking problem. His face mauled, one cheek barely hung on, and some teeth showed where flesh had once been. The guy lunged out at him, jaws snapping wildly. Tyler kicked himself away and jumped back to his feet. He took off, running full speed around the corner towards the cafeteria area. He stopped once he got there to catch his breath. The undead intruder came down the hallway towards him, he could hear him. Tyler reached for his phone, but he must've lost it in the scuffle. Realizing he had lost his phone he jammed his hand into his pocket searching for his car keys.

"Fuck!" he said to himself as he realized his keys were in the security office. The moans from down the hallway were growing closer, so Tyler took off across the auditorium foyer, stumbling up the last step in the dark. He regained his balance and made his way around the corner into the commons area of the school when a giant crash of glass erupted from the gym area, followed by what sounded like multiple moans and groans.

Is this really happening he thought, a fucking zombie apocalypse? The idea of it both excited and terrified him as he pushed through the security office door. Frantic, he fumbled around on the desk in the dark until he felt his keys and grabbed them. The groans seemed to be getting closer as he made his way out of the office and towards the front doors. He was right, in the commons seven or eight zombies milled around. One of them immediately turned in his direction as he pressed the metal door open with a squeak. The zombie burst out of the pack in a full sprint towards him. Tyler didn't hesitate as he turned himself and took off running out the doors into the parking lot.

Tyler froze as soon as he hit the asphalt making up the parking lot. There were undead everywhere across the lot. He made a break for his car. Several of the zombies took notice and closed in. Tyler forced his door closed by inches as the horde started to rock his car back and forth violently. They smacked and grabbed at the windows smearing blood and gore all over the place. He put the key in the ignition and cranked it. The car roared to life. He sped off towards his apartment complex, the entire town erupting in chaos. People ran through the streets as the zombies attacked. Tyler got so distracted by it all he took his eyes off the road and plowed into the back of a police car sitting in the middle of an intersection. With a smack his head banged against the steering wheel. Dazed by the blow, he struggled as he reached for the handle to open the door. He managed to finally grab it and stepped out, staggering like he had too much to drink.

He made it over to the police car and fell into the front seat. As he fumbled with the buttons, he accidentally turned on the lights and sirens while trying to get the radio to work. The person on the radio frantically went off nonstop about attacks and to find a secure place to hide. The lights and sirens blaring from the car had quickly become a beacon. Zombies swarmed the area in what felt like seconds. Tyler screamed as he felt one of them grab him by the legs and started to pull him out of the car. He rolled over and grabbed the passenger seat just as he felt more sets of hands pulling him, he knew he was losing his grip as he looked around in terror for something to defend himself with. That's when the first searing pain hit him as one of them bit down on the small of his back, then another as it tore a chunk out of his calf. From there it became non stop ripping and tearing at his flesh until he finally let go of the seat. As he was being pulled out he saw the police officer laying on the floor of the backseat covered by a neon green rain coat. "I'm so sorry" he mimed through the tears flowing down his cheeks. Tyler stared at him blankly as death consumed him.

WELCOME TO COTTONWOOD CREEK

REAR VIEW MIRROR

I looked back into the rearview mirror. That car was still following me. I tried to take a deep breath, but my heart was beating even faster. All I wanted to do was get some dinner before heading home to watch Netflix.

I looked back again. Still there. He was staring straight ahead, transfixed on me. He wore an old trucker hat with his gray hair peeking out below. Maybe he's not following me. After all, he could've had the same idea that I had-- that tacos sounded great after picking up a few items at the store.

The light turned red, and I quickly turned right. If he was following me, he'd turn when I would. I looked back again, and sure enough, there he was. It's okay-- just turn right again. I came up onto the next intersection, and turned into the parking lot. I drove around all of the cars and circled back to the lot entrance. His car did the same.

Okay, now you panic.

With my heart racing, I turned back onto the main road. I reached for my cell phone, and dialed 911. The dispatcher answered sooner than my breath could catch, and I stumbled over my words,

"Hi, yes, um, there's this guy and I think he's following me."

"Where are you located right now? Are you in a safe location?"

"I'm in my car, and I think... Um.. I think I'm on Washington? No wait, I'm on Harvey."

I kept heading south bound, towards the public library. It'd be easier for the police to find me in a known location.

"Which direction are you headed? Do you know where the local police station is, and if you could pull up there?"

"South. I'm heading south towards the library downtown. I-- uh, I'm sorry I don't know where the police station is."

"That's okay, you're doing just fine. If you're heading towards the library, I can have our closest officers head that way. Can you tell me more about this man? Is he driving a vehicle?"

I was afraid to look back; I didn't want to see his face again. My hands started shaking while holding the steering wheel. "He's just staring me down. He's been following me ever since he was behind me in line at the store over on Washington. I didn't notice he was behind me until I saw him at the Taco Shop."

"Can you tell what he looks like, or what kind of vehicle it is?"

WELCOME TO COTTONWOOD CREEK

I could never forget his face. "It's an older guy. I think he might be in his 60's...maybe? I'm not sure. He's got gray hair under his trucker hat, and, um... The car is like a normal car. It's silver and I think it's like a Chevy? A Malibu? I'm sorry I don't really know, it's the car behind me."

"That's okay. One of my officers should be nearing you. Are you almost to the library?

"Yeah, I'm a couple of blocks away."

"Good. I'm going to have you stay on the line with me until the officer has that guy away from you. Okay?"

"Oh my gosh, okay, thank you!" Help was coming.

I tried looking back for the cop who was supposed to be nearby, but I couldn't see them.

"You're welcome. Can you tell me anything else about this man that might help the officer more?"

"Yeah! He's wearing an orange shirt, and I think.... Yeah, it's one of those Hawaiian print ones."

I saw the red and blue lights. They were right behind him. I turned into the library parking lot, distancing myself away from that guy and the cop.

"The cop pulled him over, and I'm at the library. I'm gonna park."

"Okay, great. Another officer should be there any minute. Will you be okay if I disconnect the call?"

"Yeah, I'll be fine, " I lied. I tried watching out of the window to see what the cop was doing, but I was shaking so bad I couldn't focus. After the longest five minutes of my life, another cop pulled into the library lot, and headed over to me. I rolled down my window, hoping they knew why he was following me.

"Hey, I'm Officer Brian. I heard you haven't had the best day."

"Not exactly, no."

"We're gonna try and make this better for you. Do you have any idea why that man was following you? Have you ever met him before?"

"No... I had never interacted with him before now."

"Alright... let me go check over there and see what's going on." The cop walked back towards the street, where the other officer had pulled the guy over.

I can't believe this. I knew the cops had the guy, but it didn't help me from panicking. What did I do? Had I met him before and forgot?

I sat there in my car, leaning my head back against the seat. I tried slowing my breathing by taking slow, deep breaths. I don't think it was working.

WELCOME TO COTTONWOOD CREEK

Officer Brian made his way back towards me. I held my breath his entire walk over. "Hey. So... I can't believe I actually have to ask this, but, are you in the CIA?" My heart skipped a beat.

"The CIA? Why are you asking that?"

Officer Brian shook his head. "It's what he's saying. He told us you're an undercover agent who planted bugs in his car and his house."

"Holy shit. What? No. I'm not in the CIA. I'm a barista for Brew-Ti-Ful."

"Oh we figured he was lying. We are concerned because he's got some rope in this car... Can I see your I.D. real fast?"

I scrambled for my wallet in the passenger seat. The damn license always got stuck and would never come out when I needed it to. "Yeah, hold on, I'm so sorry."

"Are you shaking? Oh hey, it's alright. We've got him. You were so brave and right to call us."

I smiled, inhaled, and finally pulled the license out. "I'm glad you believe me, " I said, handing the license out.

"Well, in our line of work, we typically believe the scared younger women who's been clearly followed by an older male." He turned back towards his patrol car, but didn't make it far before the yelling started.

"STUPID BITCH!" The guy yelled, opening up his car door, and started shoving the officer near him. "I TOLD YOU SHE BUGGED ME. SHE GOT INTO MY HOME. MINE."

My heart started racing again. Why are you doing this?

Officer Brian ran towards the other officers, and helped with the struggle the man was causing.

"LISTEN TO ME." Officer Brian held the arms back of the man, while the other two worked to get him in the back of a car. I couldn't stop watching.

Officer Brian soon came back over to me, and brought my license back with him. "At least now we can definitely get him with assaulting an officer. Are you okay?"

I looked back down at my shaking hands. "I will be, he just... he caught me off guard."

"Understandable. And, you're sure you've never met this guy, even without being in the CIA? His name in Vonn Jones."

"No... I've never met him."

"I'm going to give you my card. You shouldn't see any more of this guy.. We'll get him taken care of for you. " I took his card, and thanked him. Officer Brian made his way back to the other police officers. I rolled down my window, thinking about how horrible that was... He never should have recognized me.

I sat there for what seemed like forever, waiting on the cops to haul him away. Once they were finally gone, I sighed, and threw my cell phone in the passenger seat. Reaching across, I opened the glove compartment. I grabbed the only item, a cell phone, and slammed it back shut. I unlocked the screen, and called the only number in the contact list.

"He's been taken care of."

WELCOME TO COTTONWOOD CREEK

Caution: Slippery When Wet

Thirty goddamn-fucking-bucket-sliding years I've been sweeping, mopping and polishing this floor. And do they appreciate it? Do they fuck! Richard thought. *They just call me names like Dickie-Slip or Slips for short!*

As the voice inside his head droned on, Slips continued to pull chairs and tables away from the fixed benches inside the restaurant. Once satisfied, he swept the cleared area of debris – stale food, napkins, straws, crayons, cutlery and other bits of shrapnel – into a neat pile before brushing it all into a dustpan and then disposing of it into a black bag.

Before putting all the tables and chairs back, he inspected that area – this section of *his*, not *theirs*, was clean. Squinting, he bent over and took a better look. *Got to make sure she's all clean today, what with it being the last day on the job. Not that they are sacking me...*he thought, a smile creeping onto his face as he looked over at the manager's coffee pot next to the bar.

Oh, they're going to pay!

Standing up straight, happy that his girl's grooves and lines were spotless, he replaced all the chairs and tables to their correct positions, mindful not to scratch his baby. In all the years he'd worked for the restaurant – Big John's Big Sloppies -- he'd not once inflicted a scratch, gouge or dent in his woman.

He took care of her, just like any man would take care of his woman.

Respect cost nothing. Zippo. Zilch. Zero. Nada.

Do they respect you? he asked, looking down at the mottled brown flooring. Do they bollocks! Damn children, the lot of them. Back in the day, when I first started tending for you, the managers had reverence for the both of us. They wouldn't come in early and track muddy boot prints right through the place. If they ever did, they had the utmost admiration, as they apologised. Not this new-aged lot, with their texting, internet on the go and Mochas!

Looking at the clock mounted on the wall behind the bar, Slips saw that it was almost ten to six. At seven o'clock, the managers would be at the restaurant to open up. Back in the day, it used to be eight o'clock, giving him plenty of time to sweep and mop – that meant the floor would be bone dry before anyone got there.

That way of working had been perfect for Slips, as by the time they used to come in, he was in the toilets cleaning out – dusting, polishing the mirrors, disinfecting the pans, etc...At that hour of the morning, the restaurant side of his cleaning job was finished, and so he was out from under everyone's feet.

Eight o'clock.

A perfect time for the others to start.

There was no need for anyone else to be there that early, considering the place didn't open until nine o'clock.

The fuckers do it to annoy! I'm positive of that.

He could hear them mocking him now: 'It's only wood, Slips! Don't be so sensitive!' *Danny, the top manager, would say.* 'Yeah, Slips – why have you got such a stiff cock for it? You take your job too seriously. You're just a cleaner!' *Trevor, the deputy manager, would chime.*' You need to get yourself a piece of arse!' *Carl, who was training to be an area manager, would constantly rib.*

"Fucking dildos! The bag of dicks wouldn't know a hard day's work, even if it bit them on the nose," he said with vitriol. Every word unleashed sounded as though it was fired from the bottom of his guts with a great deal of firepower – like a shell being blasted from a tank's turret.

He took another glance at the coffee pot. *That stuff will kill ya!* A harsh laugh burst from him as he continued to move chairs, stools and tables. He got his brush into every nook and cranny – no section was left untouched, checked and taken care of.

It was a she, and she was his lady.

I mean, you wouldn't fuck with another man's wet woman, would you?!

His thoughts had never been this dark. Hell, they'd *never* been dark. Richard Gregory Sullivan had always lived by the book in a sturdy way. He was a straight-laced, ex-military reserve. When he wasn't cleaning at John's, a job he cared for deeply, he spent his time at the beach walking his dogs, doing crosswords or pottering at his allotment.

When Joan, his wife of thirty-five years, had been taken from him by cancer, something broke inside him.

All hope, reason and care faded by the day.

And, with the world changing around him, it all helped shape a different Richard. A meaner, darker one.

Where he'd once been a willing giver and helper, now he was an expert taker; he'd never been one for being pushed around, but now he made his feelings known.

He found it hard to give respect to those in power who didn't deserve it, didn't earn it – who treated him and his work like shit. Before the 'teens' started running the show, Richard had got on well with his managers.

But not now. For the last year, he'd been subject to borderline bullying.

They may think I've been taking it on the chin, but no--I've just been biding my time, waiting for the right moment to strike. Isn't that right, Floorence? he thought, looking down at her.

When the floor was completely swept, he took ten minutes to walk around the restaurant. Slips strolled up the aisle that contained the booths and checked under the tables – all the corners were clean.

"Excellent!" He then checked under all the other tables and chairs before finally inspecting the bar area. The coffee pot caught his sight once again.

Bleach! His mind raced as he looked at it. I don't think I have much left. Not that I'm going to need it. Last day today, remember?!

Sighing, he checked the wall clock. It was almost eight.

Nodding, he grabbed his brush and made his way to the backroom. Once there, he went to his cleaning cupboard. He removed two large plastic buckets – one red, for the toilets, and one blue, for the restaurant floor.

He filled them both with water and the correct liquid. Satisfied, he grabbed the mop and took it, along with the full buckets, out to the restaurant.

The clock ticked over to eight.

Any minute now...

Plonking the buckets down, he put his mop to one side. *I won't need that just yet.* Going to the coffee pot, he lifted the lid and whiffed the contents inside. *Mmm!* he thought, replacing the lid. *It's going to be delicious!* He laughed again.

"I'm going to miss you, old girl!" he said, looking at the floor. "I hope the next person treats you as well as I have."

The spot he was looking at glinted in the light.

"No need to wink at me. I've enjoyed every minute we've spent together."

From where he stood, he traced the floor – not a dirty mark could be seen. Yesterday, he'd taken his time in giving it a second mop, after the managers had once again carelessly walked all over her wetness. Once she'd dried, Richard had polished her.

"The fuckers won't muddy or hurt your feelings again, baby!"

At five past eight, Danny, Trevor and Carl turned up at the door – the locks disengaged. Danny, who led them in, was a tall, fat lad for his twenty years. He constantly looked grubby with his food-stained shirt hanging out at the back of his trousers – this crude fashion statement of his usually ended up displaying his sweaty arse-crack every time he bent over.

If you got too close, you could smell his body odour and see the damp patches under his armpits.

He was a chunky, useless slob who found everything funny. The waitresses, who he treated like something he'd scraped off his boot heel, had named him Chuckles.

More like Wally! Slips thought, watching Danny enter John's.

"Morning, Dick!" he said with a smile, which exposed his grotty teeth – bits of food could be seen stuck in the slender culverts between them.

Slips turned his head to one side and didn't bother replying.

"Fine, be like that!" Danny said, then muttered "miserable cunt" under his breath.

"Excuse me?!" Slips bit back.

But Danny ignored him, as he made his way to the coffee pot.

"Morning, Slippy!" Trevor said. "No wet floor signs today? If anyone falls and breaks their neck, it'll be on your head!"

Again, Slips ignored the greeting. It shows how much notice they take! I haven't used the 'Caution: Slippery When Wet' signs in months. What's the point? Walk all over my baby they are going to anyway.

"Haven't you started mopping yet? You lazy shit!" Carl said. "We're going to be open in an hour, old man. Chop-fucking-chop!"

"Sorry, I'm just a bit behind this morning. My back, it's playing up," Slips said, giving it a rub. "I've normally started by now, as you well know. Disappointed you can't track through my wet floor?"

"Pardon?!" said Carl, who had started walking away.

"Nothing. Sorry, Carl," Slips said, bowing his head and looking at his feet.

Carl, who was only nineteen, was the smallest man in the restaurant. The rest of the staff, apart from Danny and Trevor, thought Carl suffered from SMS – Short Man Syndrome. His face looked like a badly topped pizza.

"I should think so, too!" Carl said. "Now get mopping."

"Can you believe the mouth on him?!" Trevor said.

As all three men congregated around the coffee pot, Slips moved to the main door and engaged the locks. "I wouldn't want anyone disturbing me, now would I?" He muttered.

WELCOME TO COTTONWOOD CREEK

"I wish we could just sack the motherfucker!" he heard Danny say.

"Agreed," Trevor said. "He's been here that long, that I'm sure they built the place around the old fuck."

Carl laughed.

In the background, the coffee pot bubbled.

Cups and spoons could be heard rattling.

With the outer door locked and bolted, Slips backed through the inner door and did the same.

Nobody was going anywhere.

"Did you just lock the doors, Slips?!" Danny asked.

"Yeah, I'll unlock them once I've mopped this area. I don't want people walking all over my floor," he said, and then muttered, "Especially you pricks!"

"Him and his fucking floor!" Carl said.

"He probably wanks his tits off to the sight of it when we're not here in the morning!" Danny said.

"Sick old fuck!" Trevor said.

Where's the harm in a man loving his work...?

When he saw them filling their mugs with coffee, he smiled, grabbed his bucket and mop, and moved closer. He wouldn't want to miss the show.

"Before you start drinking, fellas, there's something I need to show you," he said.

"What now?" Danny snapped.

"Wait here, I'll go and get it. It's pretty damn important."

"Hurry up, then!" Carl said.

Without another word, Slips disappeared into the back again.

A few moments later, he reappeared in a heavy-duty apron, which covered most of his body. He also wore thick gloves that extended beyond his elbows. On his face, he wore something that resembled a welder's mask.

As he walked over to the three men, they burst out laughing.

"What the fucking hell, Slips?!" Danny said.

"It's the Rubbernator!" Carl said, trying to take a mouthful of coffee.

Trevor bent over with laughter.

Stopping by his bucket, Richard flipped the lid of his mask up to reveal a big, cheesy grin. "At least you arseholes are going to die smiling!"

Trevor stopped giggling and stood bolt upright. "What?!" he said.

"Oh. Nothing!" Flipping the mask back down, he grabbed his bucket and raised it off the floor. "You should have brought umbrellas!" he said, which came out muffled.

"Huh!" Danny gasped. "What's in the--" Carl said, but Slips cut in.

WELCOME TO COTTONWOOD CREEK

"Hydrofluoric acid, son – this shit will cut through ceramic. Enjoy!" he then threw the contents of his bucket over the three of them.

The majority of the acidic tidal wave washed over Danny and Trevor, with mere splashes finding Carl.

"Argh! My fucking eyes!" Danny screamed a high-pitched scream. He sounded like a little girl as the acid melted through his epidermis, then dermis, before finally stripping him back to the hypodermis – his blood vessels popped and burst like water balloons. The crimson liquid, which sizzled and spat, mixed in with the yellowy fluids. They ran off his face and gathered on the floor below him.

As Danny stumbled around, he crashed against the jukebox, which brought it to life. "Disco Inferno" boomed out of the speakers, which brought a smirk to Slips' face.

Danny rebounded off the music box and collapsed against the bar. His head resembled a melting ice cream cone. He'd stopped screaming and moving. Acid continued to trickle down his body, eating through his clothes and flesh.

Trevor, who was in an equally messy way, was crashing into tables and chairs. Cutlery clattered onto the floor. Where he'd used his hands and forearms to try and wipe the Hydrofluoric off his face, it had chewed through his limbs – the bones beneath were glistening under the ceiling lights.

His screams were wet. Soggy.

After pin-balling into another table, he fell on top of it. His shell was a sizzling, smoking wreck. Sludge, which had once been his face and arms, pooled under him.

Slips didn't have time to watch Trevor die, as Carl, who seemed like he was making a run for the door, distracted him.

"Get it off me!" he yelled. Only a portion of the right side of his face had been hit – his ear was nothing but a running mess. "It's scalding!" he cried. Grabbing the second bucket Slips had brought in, Carl dumped the contents over him, thinking it was filled with water.

But no.

Slips had also filled that one with acid, just in case he needed more...

Carl's end was brutal. His whole body was drenched in the searing acid.

Slips didn't bother standing to watch the youngster run around flaying his arms and slipping in his friends' goo.

Instead, he went out back, grabbed his 'Caution: Slippery When Wet' signs, and placed them about the restaurant.

SETTLING IN

Jenna hated the fact that no one believed her. That they all told her she needed to get used to the new noises of her new house. Even her own mother was telling her she was just being paranoid and laughed it off. Not Jenna though, something about this new house felt wrong to her. She had fallen in love with it when they looked at it, sure, but staying here when she was home alone wasn't right. She could feel it in her bones. Her husband Brian teased her relentlessly about her feelings. What worried her the most was, when she was with Brian, nothing seemed out of the ordinary at all. Soon after, on the days he left for work, the scary feelings of being watched and followed overcame her like a tidal wave. It would happen at night too, so Jenna made a habit of always going to bed at the same time as Brian, even if it meant staying up late watching him play video games with his buddies. She refused to go upstairs at night alone.

As the days passed, her feelings never changed. She couldn't stand to have her back in one direction for very long without feeling like someone was sneaking up behind her or was standing there watching her. She also never turned the volume up on the TV too loud, and she wouldn't dare put on a pair of headphones.

As more days passed the weird occurrences started to amplify, yet she felt like the boy who cried wolf because no one believed her.

One Wednesday morning after Brian had left for work, Jenna took a shower. The door rattled and she almost slipped and fell on the slick tub bottom when it happened, yet even she tried to convince herself it was probably nothing.

A couple nights later, on a Saturday night, Jenna and Brian came home from a date night horny and ready to go. In the midst of some powerful love making they switched positions to put Jenna on top, because that's what Brian liked, but when she did she couldn't take her eyes off the bedroom door.

She knew they had closed it, they always closed it. Brian, ironically who didn't like being in the bedroom with the door open, always made sure to.

She felt exposed sitting atop him naked, like someone was staring at her from the doorway watching them.

That of course lead to another massive argument between them when she couldn't continue, bruising Brian's ego.

The following Monday Brian had overslept and rushed out the door. Jenna still laid naked in the bed from the night before where she made up for the previous night going the extra mile for him, and she too was still exhausted.

She dozed back off laying there which was uncommon of her these days and woke back up a couple of hours later frozen in fear and paralyzed.

She was laying in the bed still, completely naked, all the blankets pulled back, sprawled out on her back. It felt as though someone had been touching her while she slept, like that freshly fucked feeling.

Too frightened to even reach down for the sheet to cover herself with, she sat up on the bed, pulled her knees to her chest, and put her back to the wall. After what felt like hours she finally leapt from the bed and grabbed Brian's shirt from the night before that was on the floor and put it on.

She continued her beeline for the bedroom door but when she grabbed the knob to exit it didn't budge. It was like it was locked from the outside.

She rushed back to the bed to grab her cell phone off the bedside table only to realize she must've left it downstairs last night when things got heated up on the couch.

Jenna's fear was overtaking her when the creak of the bedroom door broke her concentration. She spun to see the door standing wide open now.

"Fuck this place!" She thought to herself as she ran out the door and down the stairs into the kitchen hunting for her car keys. That's when it started.

"Thump! Thump! Thump!"

The sound grew louder as it made its way down the stairs. The sounds were slow and deliberate. When she heard the final thump and groan of the floorboard at the bottom of the staircase she was too terrified to look.

Instead, Jenna grabbed her entire purse and made a mad dash for the back door! She grabbed the knob to run outside when she was stopped, something had a hold of her by the arm and it was causing her intense, burning pain.

She cried out as she twirled around and found the apparition of an old man staring at her with such terrifying intensity she began bawling and begging for him to leave her alone.

The old man didn't let go, he never broke his stare upon her when suddenly he shoved her against the wall and took her chin in his hand looking into her eyes with the darkest, soulless eyes one could imagine and spoke to her.

"You're mine now, all mine, I've marked you on the inside."

WELCOME TO COTTONWOOD CREEK

    He spoke deliberate and slow. Jenna felt his cold hands close around her throat as he spoke, tightening his grip as she struggled to breathe.

    She was helpless and soon after she was lifeless as her body fell to the floor. Jenna stood there with the old man looking down at her former self as he gently placed her hand in his.

    "Come meet the family now." He politely spoke the words as Jenna, timid as a woodland creature, turned with him to face over a dozen women with the same soulless, blackened eyes.

    "We're all family now!" They all screamed at once as they swarmed her with her widened faces.

WELCOME TO COTTONWOOD CREEK

UNCAGED

"Fuckin' po-pos here right now, but they 'bout to leave," my sister said, slurring as usual. "They gonna get his ass. Bet. He can't run forever. They know where he lives, and they out searchin'. Bitch-ass mothafucka."

Goddamnit. "I'm on my way." I ended the call before she could respond and stumbled to the bedroom, mind racing. Hell, we'd all hung out just a few nights prior. This didn't seem like the Cage I knew. We'd even worked together for the past few years, and he'd never shown an inclination toward woman beating. Maybe it was another one of Jazzy's 'cry wolf' moments. But maybe it was legit for once. There had been rumors from his ex, who'd come in to work many times with black eyes...

My wife sat up in the bed when I flicked the light on. Her voice was monotone. "Who was that?"

"Jazzy. Cage just beat her ass."

Carrie rolled her eyes. "Like Trent did?"

"According to her, even worse." I swayed, and Carrie's soft brown curls danced with me. "Cops are there, but she's worried he'll come back. She wants me to swing through."

"You're drunk."

"It's only a few blocks away."

Carrie raised her eyebrows and stared at me. Sleep perched on her pupils like a black hole, sucking me in.

I shook myself into one-quarter sobriety. That damn DUI. Carrie would never let me live it down. "I've got feet." I turned away and headed for the hallway, speaking over my shoulder. "I'll be back in an hour or so." Her mumbled reply was consumed by my echoing heartbeat. I wobbled through the kitchen and living room, yanked the front door open, and stepped outside. A chill rippled through me. I pulled my hoodie tighter around my neck. It's too cold for this shit. And late. And dark.

But family....

I stopped beside my car and sucked in a deep breath. A strange anxiousness rippled through me. What the fuck was I thinking? Walk six blocks at midnight, inebriated, and what, stand around for moral support? If Cage returned after the cops left, I'd be as effective as a sieve gathering rain water. I didn't know the first thing about fighting. Violence wasn't in my nature.

I stared at my raggedy-ass Cavalier and smiled. Then I opened the front passenger-side door and reached into the cubby on the frame. My fingers wrapped around the miniature screwdriver I'd stored as an impromptu weapon during my pizza delivery days, and I felt invincible.

Maybe I wasn't a fighter, but I'd sure as fuck stab anyone who came at me.

I shoved it into my hoodie pocket and slammed the door shut. I'd probably pissed off a few of my neighbors with the racket I'd made, but I didn't care. We were the quiet ones in the trailer court. One night of noise could be overlooked. Besides, it was a Friday. Fuck 'em.

I rushed around the front of our trailer, hit the sidewalk, veered left, and broke into a power-walk. Tiny wisps of vapor exploded in front of my face as I marched toward Jazzy's place. Though I'd had more than my usual intake, I was alert, primed, pumped, and my vision remained clear as houses and street lamps passed by.

A large vehicle cruised past when I was two blocks from Jazzy's. I prayed it was Cage's SUV. I hoped he'd pull over and jump out, crazed, looking for retribution because Jazzy had called the cops. The adrenaline would see me through. I was certain of it

It was an SUV, but it had a light rack on top. One of the cops leaving her place. Shit. This one was for real. I picked up my pace, exerting every muscle in my body. Minutes later, I reached Jazzy's pad. Two more SUVs set against the curbs, and light spilled from the front entryway onto the disheveled yard. I heard voices coming from the house as I crossed the street. One was unmistakable but the others were indistinct.

I hopped onto the sidewalk, fingers still clutching the screwdriver, and approached the open door. Before I crossed over the threshold, I cupped my mouth and nose with my free hand and exhaled into my palm. My breath was sour and pungent from the 12-pack of Budweiser I'd consumed. Fuck. If I had to get close and personal with the five-ohs, I was certain they'd slap me with some charge or another.

But it was too late to turn back.

I didn't bother rapping on the frame, but I did announce myself. "Jazzy?"

One of the cops whirled around, hand at her hip holster. "Who's this?"

"That's my brotha. My mothafuckin' brotha. Tol'ju he'd come. That's my mothafuckin' brotha, man." The cop eyed me from head to foot. Probably convinced I was harmless judging by my nerdy appearance, she then turned back toward the pool table against the far wall. "Are you certain you want to press charges, ma'am?"

"Goddamn right. He ain't gettin' away with this shit."

WELCOME TO COTTONWOOD CREEK

"All right, well, we've got everything we need right now. We'll keep searching and let you know about court dates and whatnot. If he happens to come back, you call us immediately." She stepped aside and motioned to the male cop inside the living room.

As they exited, I got a good look at my sister, who was seated on the ground beside the pool table. Aside from her white-girl Bronx accent (though we'd been raised on a farm in Iowa), I wouldn't have recognized her. It looked as if a punter had used her head as a football. Goose-egg-sized lumps abounded on her forehead. One eye was swollen shut, the skin surrounding it purple, almost black already. The other was also swollen, though it wasn't closed. Red and narrowed to a slit, but not closed. Huge cuts on her lips and cheeks gleamed in the bright interior lighting. Browning blood covered the front of her white shirt, the carpet, the edge of the pool table.

My lungs hitched at the horror of it, and my grip on the screwdriver lessened. "Jesus Christ," I muttered, eyes wide. I'd seen her with a black eye here or there, maybe a busted lip, but not like this.

"That bad, huh?" I stepped closer, and the visible gashes widened, reddened. "You need to go to the hospital."

"That's what I told her too," Melanie said as she entered the living room. Long red hair billowed across her shoulders. When she shook her head, freckles bounced. "You need to listen to your brother, Jazzy."

Melanie was one of her best friends, but Jazzy secretly hated her. I couldn't stand her either. She was enthralled by gossip and participated in it of her own free will, making shit up to garner attention and self-worth. She knew everyone on the streets, and she could make or break your rep with but one lie. Regardless, I was glad to have her on my side this time. "Look at your damn face, Jazzy. You could have a fucking concussion. You need to get that looked at."

"Fuck that. I ain't goin' to no damn hospital. I ain't got the money or--"

"Who cares about money? Christ, you could die in your sleep!" I said.

She shook her head. "I ain't goin' to sleep tonight, man. Not with him out there." She looked up at me with her slit-for-an-eye. "Tol'ju I was fucked up, huh?"

I paused, wondering if it was a bad time for humor, then let my inebriation reign supreme. "Bad isn't even close. You look like fucking Quasimodo."

She offered what could've been a smile, though it was difficult to tell with all the healable deformities.

"That's fucked up, bro."

"It probably would've been worse, but I chased him off," Melanie interjected, her need for attention outweighing Jazzy's need for medical attention.

Jazzy scoffed. "Shut up, ol' stank-ass bitch. You didn't do shit."

Melanie turned and rushed to the kitchen entryway. She hefted a thick wooden bat in her hands and wheeled around, fiery hair disheveled. "If I wouldn't have remembered I had this behind the door, he might've kicked your skull in."

"But you didn't even get that shit 'til after he done beat me, you dumb bitch!"

"What the fuck was I sposta do, Jazzy? Look at me, and look at him. There's nothing I could've done!" She was right. She was about a third the size of Cage and a foot shorter. It would've been like unleashing a Chihuahua on a Doberman.

"You coulda done somethin' when he was kickin' my fuckin' face in!

"Whoa, whoa, wait a sec," I interrupted. As much as I enjoyed watching Jazzy knock Melanie down a notch, bickering wasn't going to do any good. "He kicked your face?"

"Cam, he fuckin' busted down the door! I was sleepin' right there"--Jazzy pointed at the couch behind me--"and he jus' came in and grabbed me up by my throat. Tossed me into the pool table. I slipped off the side onto my head, and this nigga goes and kicks my face, Cam. Kicks. My. Motha. Fuckin'. Face. Several times." She glared at Melanie with her slit-eye. "An' where the fuck was you? Over there, screamin', not doin' shit. Not 'til I was almost fuckin' dead. And that lil' bitch-ass dude you was talkin' to didn't do shit either. Lil' pussy-ass."

Melanie didn't respond, but her cheeks reddened as the remainder of the story unfolded.

Jazzy had passed out early that night before making plans with Cage. (I was certain the copious amounts of pills and weed she'd consumed throughout the day had added to her exhaustion.) Melanie had a guy friend over, and they were watching a movie in the living room while Jazzy slept. Cage had texted Jazzy a dozen times, asking what she was up to. She showed me the texts, and I could see his anger rise as more exclamation points and capitalized letters hit the screen. Because she hadn't answered, he must've assumed she was up to no good and came over to check up on her.

In the final text he'd sent, he said he heard a male voice inside and accused her of cheating and called her a slut. He must've heard Melanie's buddy, and that'd set him off. It still didn't seem to fit his character, even hearing it all, seeing it all. But people often held darkness deep inside, and it was only a matter of time before it became uncaged.

Two hours later, after helping Jazzy and Melanie secure the front door enough to shield the outside elements from coming in, I told them to call if he came back and took off for home, sober.

The whole walk there, I held the little screwdriver in a death-grip, eyes darting.

***

Monday arrived, and I headed in to work. I'd dreaded it the remainder of the weekend. Though we didn't work in the same department anymore, chances were Cage and I would run into each other eventually. Especially since he'd posted bail after getting arrested on Saturday.

I didn't dread it in the sense that I'd be afraid around him. The whole situation had stewed and marinated in my mind over the weekend, producing a boiling pot of anger and unbridled fury. I dreaded seeing him because I was afraid of what I'd do.

I'd run through it a million times: I could print off the arrest record from the weekend paper and plaster it all over the cafeterias so people could see what kind of monster he was. Taint his rep. Destroy him by word-of-mouth. But that was the nice dream. The other one entailed grabbing one of the thousands of box cutters on the floor in the warehouse, finding him inside a trailer on the dock, catching him off guard, cutting the dock light off and casting the trailer into darkness, beating him down (we were about the same size, and I was confident I'd hurt him), slicing, stabbing.

But alas, stark reality had prevailed over twisted daydreams. I had a wife, a toddler. I was a member of management. I had a clean record (except for my DUI). I didn't need that kind of rap on my sheet no matter how much I wanted to see him suffer for what he'd done to my baby sister. I had to rely on local law enforcement to serve justice.

I had to keep my inner monster caged.

For the first couple hours of the day, I ignored the incessant roiling within my gut. I kept my head down and stayed focused, or chatted with my associates, trading theories about the latest Game of Thrones cliffhanger. Whatever it took to keep my mind off the weekend's events.

When it was time for our daily morning management meeting, the turmoil inside my belly amplified. Our meeting room was near the docks.

WELCOME TO COTTONWOOD CREEK

Where Cage worked. And, like clockwork, their first break of the day tended to coincide with the adjourning of our meetings. I would likely see him. And I would be powerless, crippled by my lifestyle and career, bound by cold chains of rationality.

I would have to be Melanie, standing off to the side with a baseball bat, watching from the sidelines. During the meeting, I fidgeted so much my boss, Betty, asked me into her office afterward to find out what was bothering me. I didn't check the clock, but I was thankful for the open door. It meant I could avoid seeing Cage, avoid the burning ember of hatred which had manifested deep within.

Betty had always been my rock at work, the one I could vent to without repercussions, and she could read me better than anyone else. Comfortable with being myself in her presence, I blabbed the whole situation to her, and she listened intently, as always. By the time I was finished, I shook with rage. She offered sage warnings and advice about keeping it professional in the workplace, effectively calming me down. Then she stated she had another meeting to attend, and I headed back toward my corner of the warehouse, my sanctuary from the impure thoughts wreaking havoc on my gray matter.

I waltzed through the hallway calmer yet still on edge, and passed the cafeteria. It buzzed with activity, and something wrenched the pit of my gut. I should've checked the goddamn clock. It was break time for the unloaders.

Coworkers filtered out from the cafeteria, converging in front of me. I held my breath, eyes forward, steps mechanical and rushed. Then I breathed a sigh of relief. Cage wasn't one of the people ahead of me. I could make it past without having to see his ugly face.

But then my senses heightened, and I felt eyes boring into me. I glanced at the stream of people still filtering out from the cafeteria.

We locked gazes. Anger radiated from his eyeballs as much as it did from mine, and a red haze hijacked my clear vision. Why the fuck was he mad? What the hell had I done to him? Was he suffering from that much guilt?

Everything my boss had said flitted away into the ether, replaced by the scenarios I'd run through over the weekend. But then I remembered my wife, my son, my life, and the hostility melted, shrinking down to a tiny inconsequential lump of defeat.

Cage had me, and he knew it. He knew I'd been building my life up, had worked hard to get where I was, and violating the company's rulebook in regard to workplace violence would destroy the foundation of my life.

He knew I was a Melanie, standing idly by, powerless.

Still, I wasn't going to back down from such flagrant displays of alpha-male attitude. I slowed my pace, not breaking our eye-lock, and allowed him and his little laughing cronies to get in front of me. His bright orange shoes glowed like a beacon, holding my sole focus. He craned his neck left and right as we headed onto the floor, as if nervous about me being behind him.

A wicked sneer split my lips. Good. I was okay with him looking over his shoulders. It was the least bit of legal revenge I could get without sacrificing anything.

But as the unloaders turned toward their area and I broke away for mine, the red haze lingered. When I got back to my desk, I grabbed one of the cheap silver box cutters and sat, stroking it, pressing the point of the razor blade into the tip of my pointer finger, relishing its sharpness. It'd be so easy...

A few hours passed, during which the internal battle for my sanity waged. I wanted to hurt that motherfucker. The cops weren't going to do shit. Maybe probation, at worst. I could take law into my own hands with but the flick of a wrist and a precise slash.

In the end, rationality once again claimed victory.

Betty called me to her office during lunch. Knowing I might have to see Cage again, I pocketed the box cutter and played with it as I walked to the other side of the building. It was reassurance, like a tiny voice, a conscience which stoked the flames of evil desire. I was certain I wouldn't use it, but it still felt good.

Cool, metallic, smooth.

I passed the cafeteria without incident, though my eyes burned a hole in the back of Cage's bald, wrinkled head. He sat at a table, guffawing, having a grand old time. Like he'd never done anything wrong. Like he was a saint.

The demon inside me rattled its cage, but I silenced it.

When I got to her office, Betty was putting her coat on.

"Going out for lunch?" I asked, trying to shake off the red haze again.

"Yes. Shawn and I are trying this new thing where we spend our lunches together during the week. Kind of rekindling the marriage, you know?"

WELCOME TO COTTONWOOD CREEK

"Sounds like a good idea. Never hurts to freshen it up every once in a while." I stood in the entryway, hands in my pockets. "So what's up?"

"That's it. Just wanted to tell you I was heading out for an hour or so"--she narrowed her eyes like my mother used to--"and to make sure you're doing all right."

I gulped. She knew me too well.

Before I could stutter my way through some form of reassurance, her cell phone rang, loud and annoying inside her cramped office. She held up a finger and took the call. She muttered a few "uh-huhs" and lines creased her forehead as the conversation unfolded. "Where at?" She gestured at me for a pen, frantic. I reached up and grabbed the one I always kept in the space between my baseball cap and my ear, gave it to her, then shoved my hand back into my pocket and wrapped my fingers around the cutter, conjuring dark fantasies involving Cage.

She scribbled an address on the paper, said a curt farewell, and ended the call. "Well, looks like Shawn will have to take a raincheck. Just got word my sister is in the hospital. Bronchitis."

I chuckled. "She's what, forty? That doesn't sound serious enough to cancel a lunch date. You don't think Shawn will be mad?"

"Bah. He knows I need to be there for her. I'm all she's got. Even if she does just have a bad cough." Betty said she might not be back before the end of the shift, mumbled a half-hearted farewell, and bustled out of the office.

I followed. The bell announcing the end of lunchtime bleeped over the loudspeakers. As I neared the cafeteria, I searched for my nemesis. Thankfully, he was nowhere in sight.

I made my way to the nearest bathroom, walked in, stepped to one of the empty urinals farthest from the stalls, and relieved myself. While my piss whizzed out in a violent stream, my mind wandered. I was the only one Jazzy had, in the same state anyway. And she'd had a string of failed relationships which had culminated in abuse and multiple 911 calls. Someone needed to do something about it. She shouldn't have to live her life in constant fear.

Would my wife understand if I did what I had to do for my family, though, like Betty's husband did? Would my son understand? Would they forgive me for losing my job and realize I'd done what I'd felt needed to be done regardless of the consequences?

I glanced down as my piss settled into a slow trickle and then stopped altogether. I shook my cock more times than was allowed before it was considered masturbation, then reached up to flush the urinal.

A glow grabbed my attention. A foot, under the nearest stall.

A bright orange-shoed foot.

No fucking way.

All the thoughts I'd had over the weekend crashed down upon me, and Jazzy's fucked-up face flashed into my mind. My baby sister, the one I'd never protected from her pussy-ass woman-beating boyfriends in the past. My blood, the one I'd whooped on a few times in my day for various reasons. The one my older brother had told me to watch and protect like a good brother should.

And just like that, the red haze lifted.

My wife was close to her family. She would understand, in due time. She would hate me--as would my son, likely--but she would understand.

Hoping he hadn't caught a peek at me through the cracks in the stall door and the mirrors across from us, I zipped my pants up and walked over to the sinks, mind abuzz. What was I going to do? Whatever it was, it'd have to be slick. A bitch of his caliber didn't deserve a fair fight. He hadn't given Jazzy that chance. He didn't deserve it either.

I cranked the faucet on, adrenaline blasting through my veins with all the power and speed of a raging rodeo bull. Then I turned it off, grabbed a paper towel, opened the door, and made a couple loud footsteps before it closed.

Quiet as could be, I stepped back toward the urinals, certain he couldn't see me in the mirrors.

A toilet flushed and gurgled, and a few seconds later, Cage emerged. He stepped to the sinks, eyes down, and cranked one of the faucets on. Then he glanced up into the mirror, and his shoulders hitched as if he'd choked on a dick.

I second-guessed myself, then shook the nagging doubts away. I'd gotten that far. It was time to step over the edge. For Jazzy.

I crossed over to him as his eyes widened, grabbed the nape of his neck with both hands, and smashed his face into one of the mirrors. Shards of reflecting glass scattered, cascading onto the porcelain sinks and skittering across the floor, shattering further. He grunted and stumbled backward. Blood gushed from his busted nose. A tooth plunked out of his mouth and clattered to the floor.

Mustering every bit of anger I'd repressed over the years, I shoved his chest. He reeled backward, crashing into the stall he'd shat in. Then I kicked, hitting him square in the balls. He gripped his shriveled sack and I stepped forward, releasing a vicious straight right which turned his face away.

Then I gripped the back of his head and forced his ugly fucking face into the stinky toilet.

I held him there, vision clearer than it'd been all day. Water splashed, baptizing me in shit-flecked water. He clawed at my hands, but I felt nothing, heard nothing.

Nothing but a cage being shaken to its core.

I released my hold. Cage's head snapped back. He sputtered and gasped as if he'd been at the mercy of his own rage. I couldn't see his face, but I imagined it was bruised and lumpy and swollen, as Jazzy's had been.

The internal cage rattled once more, and then the lock snapped like a twig and fell away, and all lingering doubts washed away in a burning, cleansing fire of relief.

My hand slipped into my pocket and withdrew the box cutter. I gripped it tight, pushing the blade out to its full extent. Without further hesitation I slashed at the exposed flesh on the back of his neck. Deep gashes appeared, more and more, and blood poured in torrents. The gashes widened. Sickening strands of muscle fiber peeked out, and things I'd never known existed inside a human body eked from the wounds. Soon, his shouts and moans and ignored pleas ended, and his body slumped to the floor, lifeless. I walked backward out of the stall. Someone opened the main door, paused, muttered something unintelligible, and then took off.

I stood there, skin and clothing stained crimson, staring at the human waste gathered on the bathroom floor. Maniacal laughter erupted from my mouth.

My inner demon, finally uncaged, laughed with me until the cops arrived.

WELCOME TO COTTONWOOD CREEK

MIDNIGHT CRUISE

Let me tell you about this one night back in the day that scarred me for life.

What a great concert! That's all the four of us could talk about on our way home after the show! Jace, Abbie, Reagan, and I had graduated from high school a few weeks ago. This trip was one of our highlights of the summer before going off to college. Jace and Reagan had dated since the eighth grade. They finally convinced each of their best friends, Abbie and I, to start dating the summer before our Sophomore year. In a couple more short weeks, we would all head to separate colleges, but tonight was one of the best nights of our lives. We all continued to gush about how great the concert had been for days after. Yet none of us ever brought up the other incident from our trip home. I have never brought it up until now.

A heavy rain started on the drive home. I regretted my decision to not replace the shitty wiper blades on my beat up old Monte Carlo, even though it still ran like a champion.

Because of the down pours I decided to head off of the interstate and take the back highway home. I figured it would be better that way, with all the small towns we would pass through, in case I needed a break from the rain or to wait out any potential heavy showers.

As we cruised along the back way, Jace prodded the girls with made up stories of murderous lore. We passed an old meat plant, which due to the haze created by the rain looked ominous and ghostly in the dark shadows. Only a couple of lights still shined down on the big vacant parking lot. The girls nuzzled in closer to us men as we traveled past it. Somewhere down the road, after passing the old plant, Abbie giggled as she prompted me to look in the rear view mirror. No wonder Jace had become so quiet, I thought to myself, as he and Reagan were locked into a full blown make out session in my backseat.

By the time we reached the town of Silver Falls everyone in the car other than myself obviously had started to nod off or was already slumbering in their seat. I decided a pit stop would be a good idea to grab some caffeine, besides I needed to take a leak anyways. I woke the other three as I pulled up to the gas pumps to top off the tank as well. All four of us stretched and groaned as we piled out of the car and into the store for our wants or needs. The others offered to relieve me of my driving duty but I declined as always, I didn't care much for anyone else driving my car.

The storms had picked up again a few miles west of Silver Falls. Visibility was not ideal between the rain and the dark, add in the terrible job the wipers were doing, and I wasn't enjoying myself anymore. I had almost lulled myself into hypnosis when Reagan's voice from the backseat zapped me out of it.

"What's that up there by the road? Is that a car?" she asked looking ahead.

"I think it might be." I answered back as we slowed down some more as we approached it.

Once we all realized it was indeed a car I slowed to a stop on the side of the road. It was a white car that had hit a culvert off the side of the road. I angled my Monte Carlo to light up the car then Jace and myself hopped out to check it out. The front end of the car was smashed to hell and the front drivers side tire had caved in and leaned at an unintended direction. Strangest of all was the fact the driver's side door was wide open but there didn't seem to be anyone around. The two of us got back in the car and waited while Reagan called 911. The dispatcher informed her they would send an available unit out to check on the abandoned vehicle. Satisfied with that answer the four of us decided as a group to head on our way.

We had only been back on the road for a few minutes, just outside of the town of Crossville, when something else came into our vision. It slumped in the middle of the two lane highway. I once again eased off the accelerator as I neared the object. What I had thought was a box in the middle of the road turned out to be a car seat. Out of stupid instinct I slammed on the brakes. That made the car loose and it felt like we were on the verge of hydroplaning, due to the wet conditions. My car skidded to a stop near the edge of the road.

Abbie was the first of our group to clamber out of the car, followed by the others. We rushed over to the seat sitting perfectly upright along the white dotted lines in the middle of the road. The seat was empty, not a trace of evidence a child had been in it at all. Jace carried it to the side of the road, and we all shielded our eyes from the rain as we strained to look around both sides of the road for any sign of distress. After a few minutes of searching the soggy surroundings, we retreated to the dry confines of my Monte Carlo.

I had gotten the car back up to speed when the woman in the white robe came into view of the headlights. She was soaking wet from head to toe and carrying a baby.

"Oh my God, we have to stop!" Both the girls cried out simultaneously.

Neither Jace nor I protested, so I let off the accelerator and coasted towards the lady. She was walking right down the middle of the two lane highway. She didn't even seem to notice we were pulling up behind her, she never quit looking ahead until we rolled up beside her. I rolled my window down and called out to her asking if she was okay. She didn't verbally respond but instead shook her head from left to right. When I tried to ask her if we could give her a ride she changed to nodding yes.

I brought the car to a stop. The woman walked around to the passenger side as Abbie got out and slid into the back with Reagan and Jace. She climbed in without a word, clutching her child tight to her chest, while patting its back and slightly bouncing it. We again tried to ask her if she was okay and again she wouldn't even look at us, she just looked straight ahead or down at her baby as the water dripped off of her. I cranked the heat on in the car and sped up knowing we were only a few miles at most from Crossville. Something about the presence of this woman in the car with us made everyone uncomfortable. She never spoke, but we all sensed something had to be wrong. The crashed vehicle and the car seat all had to be from her

It was only a few minutes later as we pulled into the city limits she started to mutter something.

"Keep going, he'll hurt you too." The chick said it over and over.

The lady started to bounce and sway the baby much more as she chanted the words. I shot my friends a quick look in the rear view mirror, and they returned my concern gaze. I found myself speeding up as I rounded a curve and saw the twenty four hour station lit up.

"Let's go inside and get you some help." I was still trying to be comforting but the lady was frigidly cold and distant.

She didn't even acknowledge the gesture, she sat there as if she had no intention on moving. I stepped out of the car and looked to the back seat as the three of my friends couldn't seem to get out of the car quick enough. Abbie retreated into my arms as Jace and Reagan joined us by our side. We offered one more attempt to get the lady out of my car with zero luck. With that we headed through the door into the shop, where we did our best to explain to the old man behind the counter what was going on. He said it would be okay and proceeded to call the police. It didn't take long for the deputy from the local sheriff's office to arrive. We again explained everything to him, the car they had found crashed, the car seat, the lady walking down the road. Honestly, I was getting tired of repeating myself for this crazy lady.

The deputy called over and asked me to come outside with him. When we approached my ride, the woman still sat there rocking in the front seat.

"Holy Shit! Get back inside with your friends." The deputy barked at me out of nowhere as he grabbed the mic connected to his radio from his shoulder.

I rushed back inside and along with the shop clerk we all watched from the windows as another police vehicle arrived, along with a white van and an ambulance. They tried to order the lady out of my car, hands on their weapons at the ready. The lady continued to ignore everything happening around her, until the man in the white doctors coat emerged from the van.

Then chaos.

She thrashed around inside the car. She climbed over into the driver's side, then started punching and shaking the wheel violently. The deputy rushed in asking for my keys and immediately went to the driver's side. He slowly made his way over to unlock the door while the lady glared at him with a terrifying scowl. She awaited the door to open and leapt out at him. The two officers wrestled her to the ground and tried to handcuff her. The man in the doctors coat approached and gave her a shot of something. It wasn't long until they subdued her. The medics from the ambulance brought over a gurney, where they strapped the lady down with leather restraints.

    The four of us continued watching as the deputy reached into the car and pulled out the baby. He unwrapped it revealing its true identity, a baby doll. Abbie and Reagan both gasped. I could feel the hair on the back of my neck tingle. The Deputy came inside and explained to us how lucky we were. The woman had escaped from a mental hospital nearby after she attacked and killed a night nurse at shift change. She had been locked away for years at the Cottonwood Creek Mental Health Rehab facility. She'd been convicted and found guilty of drowning her own child in a creek not far from where we had found her that night.

WELCOME TO COTTONWOOD CREEK

Daddy Stitch

...needles and pins, when you get married your trouble begins

... Susan clung to the words—her newborn, too-- as Doctor Lisa sewed her vagina.

"I paid--"

"...For the daddy stitch, we know," Lisa interrupted Trevor, Susan's husband, glaring at him.

"Finished, Susan."

"And..."

"In time, Trevor... Nurses, aid Neanderthal in undressing."

The two assisting nurses shoved Trevor into a chair, ripped his clothes off and tied him up. "What...?!"

"Ready for tightening, daddy? My glue will do the trick!" Lisa raised a syringe, stabbed it down Trevor's urethra and plunged the pearl-coloured liquid.

Susan smiled from behind the doctor...

WELCOME TO COTTONWOOD CREEK

THE SAGA OF JOHN ELTON

John sat at his desk in his corner office, looking out the window at the neighboring skyscrapers, a smug smile on his face. He just knew it was going to be another glorious day at work. He could feel it. That first quarter bonus would be fantastic. He wasn't sure what he would spend it on, but all those zeros on his income statement sure were nice.

Already his secretary had his schedule displayed on the big screen television up on the wall behind him. It was just perfunctory, he already knew his whole weeks schedule even though it was just Tuesday.

The day was ticking along like clockwork, just as he liked it. That's why he almost jumped when his phone buzzer suddenly went off.

What could Ms. Shelling want? "Yes!" He barked into the speaker.

"Sorry to bother you, sir." John could picture her recoiling at his anger in his mind and smiled. "I just thought you should turn on the news sir. Something strange seems to be going on."

"Thank you," he said and hung up on her. She was his newest secretary, the third this year. He would get her trained on his protocols and procedures yet.

Probably just more of that nonsense I heard on the way here.

John always listened to Fox Business Talk on the way to work. It had been interrupted two times this morning about talk of some kind of riot or something out on the East Coast. He didn't know for sure, he only half ass listened. He had no use in knowing what was going on out on either coast. That's why he lived and worked in Chicago. It was in the solid, predictable Midwest of the greatest country on the planet. He felt if he ever had to go to California, it would be like going to his own private hell.

Ignoring his secretary, he got on his computer instead and pulled up all the relevant financial files for his first client this morning. They were asking for a loan to expand their construction business and he planned on grilling them extensively before he decided. He had a nose for whether people were good solid investments or not. That's how he got where he was after sixteen years.

A knock came on his door. He glanced at the clock on the screen. His appointment wasn't due to arrive for another twelve minutes.

Letting his annoyance known he said, "Yes, come in." It wasn't his nine o'clock, it was Bob, from the office next to his.

WELCOME TO COTTONWOOD CREEK

"Can you believe the crazy shit on the news?" Bob started right in without so much as a hello or good morning.

"Bob, I have a client coming in eleven minutes. Can-"

Bob cut him off and gestured to John to come join him at the window. John annoyance went another notch up the scale. Technically John was Bob's boss. How dare he ignore and disrespect me like that?

With a huff John got up and came over. He figured he would humor Bob and later he would reprimand him.

"Down there." Bob pointed for emphasis, finger jabbing the glass.

John grudgingly looked down. The streets below were a sea of chaotic people. From this high up they were just faceless figures but John had never seen anything like he was viewing now. It seemed as if half of downtown Chicago were running wild in the streets. Cars mangled and crashed covered the streets and the sidewalks. Police cars, a fire truck or two, ambulances, these were all over the place as well. No sound could be heard so that made the scene even more surreal.

John tore his eyes away with an effort and whispered to Bob. Why he was whispering he didn't know. "Bob, what the hell is going on?"

Bob's response was to hit the remote built into John's desk to flip the channel to the local Fox news station. "It started out in New York, Boston, Baltimore, Savannah. All up and down the East Coast. That was during my commute here. How it reached us so fast..." Bob trailed off, letting the newscast take over.

"Things are happening so rapidly but we are trying to keep everyone up to date," the newscaster looked sweaty and to John it seemed as if his professionalism was being held together by sheer willpower. "Right now we are recommending that everyone stay in their homes. If one of your loved ones seem ill, quarantine them in a locked room of your home, like a bathroom. All hospitals and emergency services are at capacity or more right now so please, do not attempt to go anywhere unless it is a true emergency."

"What is he talking about? Lock your sick friends or family members in the bathroom?" John was beyond confused.

He whipped out his cell phone. He needed to call his mother, make sure she was okay. He was a little shocked she hadn't already called him. She lived right outside the Kansas City area, an even saner place than where he lived. He was sure she would be fine, but he stabbed the button to call her anyway.

WELCOME TO COTTONWOOD CREEK

He looked back out the window, watching people below scurry like frenzied ants. He saw smoke start to rise between the buildings in the distance. He kinda lost track of how long he had stood there without getting a ring tone. He pulled it from his ear and looked at it. It just sat there saying connecting. The time he had attempted connecting said 2:41 had past.

He turned around to say something to Bob, but he was gone. He didn't do Facebook or Twitter or any of that nonsense so he decided he was going to use his landline. Just as he sat down at his desk and picked up the receiver, the building shook. A rumble made the windows vibrate. Then the power went out. He looked at the phone blankly then hung it up.

He expected to hear his coworkers and subordinates talking loudly and some maybe even screaming in panic. Instead it was quiet. Too quiet.

He opened up the heavy wooden door to his office and peaked his head out into the cubicle farm.

"Hello?"

No answer.

He stood there half in, half out of his office. He had a feeling he had never experienced before. Hesitation. He couldn't decide what to do. Should he stay until things sorted out and the power came back on? Or should he leave like the rest?

The lights flickered and came back on. That settled it for him. He went back into his office. He grabbed his laptop, threw it in the case, and headed out to the elevator. He glanced up at the TV. It was a dark rectangle on the wall. He clicked it back on. Fox news came back with continuing coverage about attacks from the East Coast that were now reported as far west as Illinois and Tennessee. At the same time things had started going crazy on the East coast, the West coast was also experiencing the same thing. It wouldn't surprise me, coming from California. Now there were two talking heads, one from each coast, along with the newscaster standing in the middle. John thought he heard a word that began with z. There goes the news, sensationalizing everything again.He figured there was nothing more for him to learn from the boob tube, it was time to go. He'd be safer at home, in his secured neighborhood. It was eerily silent out in the regular office space. Just the background hum of office equipment running and the click of his Corthay shoes.

He turned right and passed out the door of Imperial PFS. He paused for a moment to lock it behind him. He was thinking about damn looters and rioters. Little shits like to take advantage when there's a crisis. He was now in the main hallway. He went right again, passing the stairway door and then took a left. He continued on then stopped. He hadn't seen or heard another person the entire way. Now he swore he could hear someone moving around behind him. He strained his ears. Yes, there was a bang against the wall and the scuffle of feet on the carpet.

John called out. "Hello? Who's there?"

The sound of a body careening off the walls quickened in intensity. John felt his heart thump louder in his chest. He turned and in not a walk, not a run, he went to the bank of two elevators and pushed the up button. He turned around, eyes scanning the hallway. He wasn't even aware that he was clutching his laptop case to this chest. Or that his breath had sped up.

A figure came into view from one of the connecting hallways. They moved like they were hurt, swaying on their feet. He almost called to the person as they stood there with their back to him, looking up the hallway. Then they turned and looked his way and John praised God that he didn't.

The person thing was a man dressed a lot like him. He had on a three piece business suit that was missing its entire left side under the armpit down. In its place John could see the man's skin with what looked like a shark bite from Jaws. John could swear he could almost see the guys liver. Funny thing was, the gaping wound was not bleeding.

John tore his eyes from the man's torso to his face. Where his left eye should've been stood an empty socket, puckered and surrounded by some kind of crimson, wet jelly stuff. John felt his gorge rise as he realized it was probably blood.

One hand went from holding his case to holding his mouth. He tried to will himself to keep calm. He didn't want to draw any attention to himself as the man thing still stood where it was, looking around but somehow it didn't seem to be zeroing in on him.

Then the elevator dinged behind John as the door opened. The thing turned its full body his direction and shambled his way. It made no noise of triumph or a wail signaling an attack. It made no sound at all, besides its body interacting with the walls and carpet.

John slid sideways towards the open elevator as the thing slid closer towards him. The thing the news said was a zombie. When his butt could feel open space behind him, he stepped backwards, unable to take his eyes off the thing closing the gap between them. He just stood there, looking at the open doorway. Waiting for the doors to close. Waiting to see if his mind would snap or not.

WELCOME TO COTTONWOOD CREEK

    The zombie was now coming through to join him in the elevator. John almost smacked himself for being a dummy and instead smacked the elevator door close button. The doors slid towards one another, bumped one of the now outstretched arms of the zombie, and opened back up. John moaned low in his chest. He stabbed the button again and again. The doors closed and opened. The zombie took another step farther inside.

    Not thinking John raised his laptop case and smashed it with all of his adrenaline fueled might on the zombie's head. Something inside the laptop tinkled and the zombie dropped. The doors tried to close once again but now the things head was in the way. Another moan, almost childlike in terror, escaped John as he drew back one perfectly polished shoe and kicked the head. It moved and John went back to hammering the close door button. He exhaled loudly when the doors shut.

    John slumped against the back of the elevator. His laptop case was held to his chest like a little kid holding their favorite stuffed animal. Something jagged extended the lining of the case in several places. Huge whooping breaths came from John as he stood, looking up at the floor display. It wasn't changing.

What the fuck? What the hell? Was the litany that repeated inside of his head. Why am I not going down?

John looked at the elevator buttons. None of them were lit up.

"Silly me," he said aloud, "need to push a button."

He reached for G. As he pushed it, something thumped against the door. John jumped back and shrieked, raising his case above his head without thinking about it.

With the whir and a small hitch, the elevator started. John stood frozen. The elevator dinged and the display went down one number. John stood frozen. The elevator dinged again. John's arms came down to his chest. The elevator dinged again. John went back to hugging his laptop. The lights flickered, the power went out and the elevator jerked to a stop. Total darkness.

Then the light overhead came back on, though it was a visibly weaker.

Maybe some kind of backup?

John felt a relieved that at least he wouldn't be sitting here in the dark. With those...things. He spent a moment trying to get his composure back. If he were rescued, it wouldn't do being found out of sorts. He slumped completely to the ground.

You're not going to be rescued, a voice spoke up in his head. Usually that voice sounded like his mother. Why didn't you take the stairs? Now you're in danger.

"I wasn't thinking clearly," he answered out loud. "Bob, the news...they spooked me."

Maybe you're not as smart as you think, huh?

"Shut-"

A thud on the top of the elevator made John skitter upright. Eyes wide, he looked up. Then he felt the elevator jerk and move again. It seemed slower but at least it was going down. John told himself that the thump was just the equipment getting him going again. Then there was another thud on the ceiling.

The display wasn't working so John had no idea what floor he was on or exactly how fast the elevator was moving. John kept quiet, straining his ears. Someone, something, was moving around up there. Then there was a third thump.

John suddenly had a panicked thought that the emergency power controlling the elevator couldn't handle as much weight as normal. He found himself reaching for the button, pushing every one of them to make it stop.

The machine lumbered to a stop and the doors inched open. A long hallway stretched before John.

Dark except for the glare of the emergency lights about halfway down.

He looked down at his watch. The face was cracked but the minutes still ticked away. *My appointment should be showing up now.* Had it only been that long since this all started? Hysterical laughter escaped from John. Then he clamped one hand over his mouth. His other still held the broken laptop. Why? He didn't know. He kept it anyway as he scuttled off the elevator. The thumping now behind him increased in volume, so he quickened his pace.

He had no idea what floor he was on or where the stairs were. He approached each bend or junction as if there was a bomb right around the corner, waiting to go off in his face.

He passed a bathroom, which led his body to remind him he really needed to go. Usually he was regular but in this case, he ignored it. He'd go when he was safe. *Or in my pants like a baby.* The laughter of a deranged man bubbled through his tightly held lips. When he felt somewhat recovered, he went on.

He eventually saw a sign pointing the way to the stairs. He followed it and another was up ahead, pointing right. He took the turn, laptop over his head. Nothing was there.

WELCOME TO COTTONWOOD CREEK

Another set of the emergency light banks were above a door close to him. That was probably the stairs. He started for them and then stopped. Coming his way was a figure. He couldn't quite see who it was in the gloom beyond the lights. Or what it was. It seemed to walk normal though. He resisted calling out. Even if he really, really wanted to.

It walked closer. He could tell now it was a woman. She had long hair, a blouse, and a skirt on. He took a few tense steps towards the door, eyes on her the whole time. She didn't call out to him but that could be for the same good reason he didn't. Or a bad one.

John inched along, bag at the ready. The woman came closer down the hallway. He reached out his hand for the handle. Still she came on. He turned it. The click as it opened seemed deafening in the stillness. He looked at the woman out of the corner of his eye. She had stopped. John had decided something was wrong with her after all. The way she stood there, tense. It was like an animal searching for its prey. Hunting.

John spun through the door, slamming it behind him. Not waiting to see if she followed him, John attacked the stairs. He had no idea how many he had gone down. When he reached the end, he was panting and sweating and cursing himself.

He hid underneath the shelf of the stairwell, sitting there trying to ignore the pain in his lungs, heart, and legs. More than that, he needed to calm his mind, so he could think. Every time he tried to get some mental clarity, his mind slid back to what was happening. It felt like his brain was teetering on a cliff, whose bottom could not be seen.

Once he felt a modicum of control, his bladder started screaming at him. He looked at his busted watch. It was way past the time he usually had his mid morning break. He painfully scooted over to the corner where, if he tilted his head just a bit, he could see out the glass door. He was glad it required a security card to get in. Panic hit him though as he wondered if that worked while the power was out.

For walking, he didn't know what else to call it, outside of that door were groups of the things. That changed his mind about escaping the building. Sure there were a few in here with him. There were by now thousands of them out there. He didn't know why he had the rush to get outside now. Panic I guess.

Instead of reaching for the door outside, John cracked open the door that led into the building. It opened on the lobby to the right and a bank of elevators to the left. In the emergency lights, John could see the sign for the bathrooms right past the elevators. He eased the door closed behind him with a barely audible click.

Feeling foolish but doing it anyway, John crept as slowly as he could across the way and down the short hallway to the bathroom. Every step was torture in more than one way. He couldn't remember a time he had to go so bad. His eyes flicked everywhere in a loop but he didn't see any movement. He passed a water fountain and opened the door to the men's room as deliberately as he had closed the stairway door. With an audible sigh of relief, he locked the door behind him.

It had been ten days so far, according to his calendar. He put the big black X through the box. He had set up "home" in the bathroom. It was a solid wood door that locked, he had access to water, and he could do all his bodily functions.

He had "stolen" the calendar not long after going into the bathroom and deciding there he would stay. John realized he had begun thinking of lots of things in air quotes lately. Like how he still hoped "help" would be coming. What that help would look like he wasn't sure. National Guard? Army? Delta Force? He didn't know. This was the United States though, surely someone was coming.

After the foray to get the calendar, along with paper and writing tools, John had only gone out to raid the snack machine across the hall in the opposite alcove. He scheduled this for every other day. It didn't take him long to come up with schedules. Starting on the second day, he would wake up. Strip, except for his jacket which he used as a pillow, and wash himself off in the sink. Once dried he would dress. If it was food day, he would go out and raid the machine. His stomach growled now with a hunger he had never felt before. He needed to stretch his supplies, he had no idea how long he could be trapped here, in his new "home." If he already had food, he would eat some.

John stood at the sink and looked himself in the mirror. Dark stubbles had grown on his chubby cheeks. It itched, a sensation he wasn't use to as he shaved his face smooth every day. Huge dark circles and bags were under his eyes. Was his bald spot even bigger? Sleeping on tile wasn't comfortable in the best of circumstances. At night, in the complete darkness, every little sound seemed to wake him.

Thirst, hunger, those weren't his biggest worries now. Besides being attacked by those things, he seemed to physically feel his "mind" slipping.

"It's just you and me pal," He said to his reflection in the mirror. "I don't even have a volleyball to talk to."

WELCOME TO COTTONWOOD CREEK

It was like being stranded on a desert island. Except instead of being surrounded by endless ocean and hungry packs of sharks, he was surrounded by endless concrete and a hungered pack of "zombies." He still couldn't think or say the word with a straight face.

He pulled himself away and began what he did at 1:00 every day. He wrote in a journal about what was happening. He had "stolen" it from the same office he got the calendar from, along with a stack of magazines to read. He was scribbling away his thoughts about how he was going to sue someone when he got out of this mess, or maybe multiple someones, when a smell caught his attention. He stood up, the leather book slapping the tile floor. He was usually so careful about making excess noise. That smell had put a new fear into him though. The fear of fire.

John looked down at the door. He didn't see any smoke coming through the cracks. That was a good sign. He pressed his ear up to the door, so hard as to be uncomfortable. He always did that before opening it and going out. He thought he could hear something, like shuffling of feet on the floor. Then something pounded on the door three times, startling John so bad that he took two steps back, tripped over the journal, and fell on his ass.

"Is someone in there? Come on, I can hear you." A woman, terror thick as concrete in her voice. She continued pleading. "Oh God, I think I've seen you go in there. You have to help me." She pounded again. "The window broke, they're coming in. They're everywhere now."

John kept still, sitting there on the floor. He started to raise his hand to the door then stopped. What was he going to do? He wasn't some hero. He didn't have any weapons. Why didn't she go to the Women's restroom. Yeah that's what I'll tell her.

Before he could shout out to the stranger, she cried "Get off me! Get-." Her words turned to shrieks of pain.

Then John could hear something out there, ripping and slurping and munching. John covered his ears with his hands and he inched away, still on his ass, to the far corner of the room.

John awoke with his head against the hard, cool tile wall. He rubbed his eyes, groggy. This isn't my regular sleeping position. Then it came back to him what had just happened. Maybe he didn't fall asleep.

Like a burglar John rose and crept over to the doorway, half bent over, listening for any hint of sound. He sniffed the air. The scent of smoke was stronger than before. He could swear it. He looked down and still couldn't see any smoke coming in.

WELCOME TO COTTONWOOD CREEK

The light was pretty dim though. The emergency light batteries were almost drained. John couldn't believe they lasted this long. He had found the on/off switch for it on day three and tried to conserve them.

John was at the door. Again he pressed his head against it. He stood there, listening and listening. He didn't know if it was minutes or hours. His ear became numb. He reached down and touched the handle. It was cool.

He was about to pull back when he heard that shuffling again, of feet against the floor. It was faint but it was there.How the fuck am I going to get out of here?

John backed away and went over to the sink. He put his hands on the edges and looked into the mirror. He wished he had a weapon. Even if he had no idea how to use one and would probably hurt himself trying. It would just make him feel more confident. He went on staring into the mirror, mulling over his problem in his mind.

When John started coughing, he had no idea how much time had passed. He put a fist over his mouth and twisted to look at the door. What he had dreaded was now here. Wisps of smoke were coming in from underneath it. That's probably why that woman came out of her hidey hole.

There was nothing to do for it. He wasn't going to stay here and die of smoke inhalation. He gathered up his things, stuffing them into the laptop bag but leaving the laptop itself behind, and shrugged on his suit jacket. He pressed his ear against the door one more time. The wood was still cool, which he was grateful for. He couldn't seem to hear anything out there. He grabbed the handle, holding it for several seconds, and braced his shoulder against it to open it.

The door dragged open slowly. John grimaced at the weight against it. He knew what that was. When it was open just enough to let him stick his head out and peek around, he took great pains not to look down.

The lobby area was full of billowing smoke of a mix of grey and light black. His visibility was that of a dense fog. John visibly began to shake. He pushed the door open enough to let his body out. He took a nervous first step. The front door or the side door by the stairs. Now another decision froze him. The front door was closer but there might be more of those things there than along the side entrance. Tense, every muscle quivering, he started his deliberate walk to the stairwell door.

The smoke enveloped him. He tried to hold his breath as much as possible. When he could no longer, he tried to muffle his mouth with his sleeve. Instantly his throat became irritated, but he held back the cough. He never stopped moving. He focused only on doing his best to see and hear through the thick haze. His eyes began to water, making it that much harder to focus. He thought he may have to start crawling soon.

He bumped into something and almost screamed. A muffled sound came out as he bit his coat sleeve. This time he did cough, doubled over, hands on his knees. This is it, I'm toast. When he looked back up, it was the stairwell door he had run into.

He opened it, went through, and pulled it closed behind him in one motion. Just as he did, a zombie slammed into it. He back pedaled, hitting the glass door behind him. He pushed it open, a whine escaping from him.

Out here the air was smoky too but the visibility increased dramatically. There was a blue Ford Taurus right in front of him, parked along the sidewalk. John pressed up against it and ducked down. He arched his neck back as he looked up at his building. He could see flames high up on the side. The building next to it was a smoldering husk. He hunkered down, paralyzed with the thought of what he should do next.

He knew he was on South Clark Street. He knew he wanted to get out of the city and get to his mother's home. He'd have to get to I-55. He had no idea how bad things were or how many of those "zombies" were out there. No idea if the police or the army were out in force, fighting them. He realized with growing horror just how little he knew about what was going on. How was he going to get out of the city alive?

He peeked out from around the car. There were no zombies in his immediate area. There were lots of dead bodies strewn around the wreckage of cars, trucks, buildings. Not as many as he would have thought. He shivered as he realized what that meant. A rattling sound echoed through the steel canyons. He thought it was the sound of gunfire. He couldn't tell where it was coming from. As abruptly as it started, it stopped. That's when John noticed something he thought he would never hear in one of the largest cities in the United States. Nothing. The silence of a tomb.

With nothing else to do, John picked the direction of the interstate. John scuttled from car to car, feeling ridiculous but doing it anyway. Work was about three hours behind him now, according to his watch. He wasn't sure how many miles that was. He couldn't go in a straight line as he wanted as it seemed at every other intersection was a couple of the undead. He ducked behind something or into a doorway, shaking, hand over his mouth to hold his breath.

Now the sun was going down and John panicked with a new thought, being out here in the dark with them. His heart suddenly felt heavy. He counted to ten, then methodically started over at one. He did this ten times. It helped him to continue on.

Up ahead he saw a string of hotels, including a Hilton. He decided he would try stopping there. He hugged the shoulder of the road, glancing this way and that as he walked with a hunch. In the distance he saw movement. Squinting, he could make out a man and a woman. They were running at full speed. Behind them a small pack of ten zombies were shuffling along after them. John stopped, tense. The two people made it away, running out of his sight. The zombies slowed and seemed to lose interest. They began just milling around, right in his path.

Great. Just great.

John looked around, wondering what he should do now, careful not to make noise. He was on a service road next to the interstate. The roar of an engine approaching surprised him. He watched as a newer yellow Camaro shot between the wreckage here and there on the interstate, heading south. The way he wanted to go. He would have smacked himself in the head right then if he wasn't worried about the sound it would make. He hadn't even thought of that. It had been years since he had driven.

The sound of the car's passing had drawn the attention of all the zombies in the area. Now about thirty of them were drifting down to the interstate. John found himself torn again. Should he go with his original plan to hole up or should he try to find a car in one of the hotel parking lots? Take it as far from Chicago as he could? The not wanting to be caught out alone at night won. He took the opportunity he had and continued on to the Hilton.

John made it to the entrance only to see through the glass doors it was barricaded on the inside by the hotel lobby furniture. As he peered inside, someone popped up from behind the check in desk, with a weapon in their hands. Looked like a rifle. It was getting dark, making it hard for John to see clearly. The person inside dressed in clothes that completely covered them, including a ski mask, and wore a hard hat on their head.

They came right up to the glass and gave a muffled shout. "What do you want?"

John looked around, nervous. He didn't like the idea of shouting. Maybe he should try another hotel.

WELCOME TO COTTONWOOD CREEK

There was a Holiday Inn right across the street. Then again, he could be with people. People who could protect him.

The person inside shrugged and began to walk away. John put his hands to either side of his face and shouted in the glass. "In. I want in. Please, don't make me stay the night out here with those things."

It was hard to tell through the glass but John thought it sounded like a woman. She came back to the glass. "What do you have as payment?"

John blinked, confused. What? She wants me to pay to get in?

Automatically John pulled out his wallet. He had two twenties and a ten. He held them up and waved them around. He could see the woman inside was laughing, even though he couldn't hear it.

"That shit's worthless now, you stupid moron" she said, after regaining herself. "You got any medicine, food, weapons? You know, useful stuff."

John shook his head no, then looked around to make sure no zombies were sneaking up on him. When he turned back, the woman had walked away, back towards the desk.

John stood there, stunned. He wanted to rant and rave. Yell at her, tell her he was someone important and he couldn't be treated like this. Then of course, he wasn't anymore. Right now, in the faint reflection he could see, he was just some middle aged, paunchy white guy, with nothing real to offer. What felt like a stone dropped to the base of his stomach as he realized this.

Slumped and defeated, he slinked off to try one of the other hotels.

John's calendar marked it took two days for him to leave the Chicago area behind. He was on his way to his mother's place. It was slow going but he figured it would be three more days max until he reached the old folks retirement villas, now that he was out of the city.

It had been a cluster fuck maze of one obstacle after another. Now that he was in the more rural area, it was smoother goings.

He had found an old brick of a Buick that started in the hotel parking lot of a Howard Johnson. Keys inside, full tank of gas. He traveled in it ever since, only stopping to sleep, which he did in the back seat of the car now, or to scavenge some food. He had done a lot of learning the last few days. One was to stay away from anywhere else there were people. He woke up every morning knowing that it was due to luck, not skill, that he was even still alive.

He tried to put a schedule back in place for himself. At least as far as sleeping times and eating times. It was just so hard to do now. Last night he had cried himself to sleep, lying in the back seat, shivering under a thin blanket he had found along the side of the road earlier that day. It was so, so hard.

His stomach rumbled. Looking down at his gas gauge, it was pointing at a quarter of a tank left. It was as good as time as any to find somewhere to fill up both. John passed a sign that read Burton's Travel Stop! Hot Food and Hot Showers! 4 miles! Sounded fine to him.

John had both hands on the steering wheel, not thinking about anything in particular, when he noticed a car flying up behind him in his rear view mirror. It was a dark blue sedan. It pulled up alongside of him. The passenger side window rolled down. He expected to see a friendly face. Instead it was the barrel of a rifle. It let out a steady tat-tat-tat as it played dot-to-dot along the side of his Buick. John freaked out, twisting the wheel to get away. He went off the side of the road and plowed into a tree. He felt the jerk of the seatbelt, pressure on his head. He heard a squeal of metal rubbing metal and someone laughing. Then it was blackness.

John groaned as he opened his eyes. He was looking at the glove box of the Buick. Why he didn't know. He sat up, his vision swaying a bit and his head protesting. He put a hand up to it. He didn't feel anything wet. He looked out at the tree now in the middle of the hood and it all came back to him.

He got out, holding his head the whole time, to survey the damage. When looking at all the bullet holes along the side of the car John had to pat himself all over. He just couldn't believe he hadn't been hit. That's when he noticed that his wallet was gone. He saw that the trunk was open. Before he even looked inside he knew that they had also stolen the meager supplies he had scrounged up. He went back, looked at the empty trunk, and then slammed the door in a rage. He let out a wordless scream. Weren't there any decent people left in the world!

Deflated and dejected, John sat back down in the Buick, staring at the hands in his lap. He could care less if the thieves were still out there. If zombies came for him, right now, he was done. He stared at his once nice, polished shoes, now scuffed and worn looking. Story of my life.

He looked up, out the cracked spiderwebs of his windshield. Surprise shaped his face. He was at Burton's. It was right there. John got out of the car, laughing until his face hurt.

**JOHN'S STORY CONTINUES IN
SAFE HAVEN:THE OUTBREAK TRILOGY BOOK 1**

WELCOME TO COTTONWOOD CREEK

BURIAL GROUND BUTCHERY

October 10th, 1990

Damon and Barry loved this stuff. Anything to do with anything scary! Coming out to the children's cemetery on this date had been on their radar for quite some time. As the story went, if you came out on this night, you'd see two ghosts. At midnight the one adult buried there, a mother, and her child, whom laid to rest next to her, would visit their grave. Every ten years it was rumored that on this date is when they would pay their visit and weep at their own graveside. The place had become such a popular spot for amateur ghost hunters and paranormal lovers in general, that they had fenced off the boy and his mothers grave with a wrought iron fence. This thwarted people from bothering the old and crumbling tombstones.

The story everyone knew or had been told was the same, back in the 1800s a mother was caring for her sick five year old son. Exhausted, one night in the middle of the night she got up to get him his medicine and accidentally given him kerosene which lead to his death. Unable to live with the tragedy she too drank the fuel killing herself.

The story alone was a sad one, it added to the major creep factor the cemetery already possessed. It was a dated place, almost all the tombstones that were still legible had death dates in the 1800s. Some people still brought out toys and left them by the gravestones. At some point over the years someone had placed bronzed children shoes around the one tree that stood in the graveyard.

Damon and Barry barreled down the old dirt road in Damon's beat to shit old gray 1978 Datsun Hatchback. The thing was a jalopy but it served its purpose. Barry rifled through the stash of cassette tapes in the glove box until he decided on one. He popped Alice Cooper's album, Constrictor, in the player and cranked it up. The opening riffs to Teenage Frankenstein filled the car, causing both dudes to headbang and shred some air guitar as they flew down the dirt road at unsafe speeds.

They hadn't even made it through the second song on the tape when Damon slowed down and pulled into the little half circle driveway outside of the cemetery. Damon retrieved his backpack equipped with a camera, flashlights, and a tape recorder from the trunk area of the hatchback and tossed one light to Barry. He didn't waste anytime turning it on and aimed it towards the entrance. The sign above the archway was a crudely made wooden

WELCOME TO COTTONWOOD CREEK

sign that read Cottonwood Creek Cemetery. Everything back here in the middle of nowhere seemed named after that dirty ass creek.

Damon and Barry, both with their flashlights on now made their way into the cemetery. Damon glanced at his watch, it read 11:46 p.m. The two guys strolled around inside to pass the time until midnight. They ribbed and prodded one another about which one of them would chicken out first if anything were to actually happen. As the clock neared the midnight hour they approached the fenced in area surrounding the mother and child. Maybe it was their minds playing tricks on them but the ground seemed to soften and sink in the closer they got to the fence. They joked about zombies popping out of the ground and grabbing them as Barry's alarm on his Casio watch chirped causing both of them a scare. Just like that it was midnight.

They stood there in silence looking around. The cool fall breeze made their perspiration feel like cold, shivering sweats. They waited around for a few minutes to no avail. So much for that legend they thought. Damon signaled to Barry by jingling his car keys that he was bored and unimpressed so the two of them headed back for the car. They got in bitching about how lame it was when something sounded like it smacked the back window of the car. Both of them jumped, accusing the other of fucking around. Then the laughter started, from outside the Datsun, the sound of a child laughing.

"Holy shit dude!!" Barry was stricken with panic as he looked to Damon, who was equally frozen with fear in the drivers seat. Barry urged him to start the car and go but there was no response. Damon sat there looking straight ahead, he slowly lifted his shaking hand and pointed out the windshield. Barry forced himself to turn his head and look in that direction. There, a short distance between the Datsun and the cemetery gates, a woman stood. Next to her what appeared to be a little boy clutched her hand tightly. The child was clad in dingy clothes, wearing a worn out GI Joe plastic Halloween mask. The woman not dressed much better, in torn up jeans and muck covered sweatshirt. She too concealed her identity with a mask that was pink and white, the look of a clown almost. They did not appear to be visitors from the grave. They looked very much alive. With his free hand the child waved to them. Without taking his eyes off the figures Damon slid the keys into the ignition. The engine sputtered but it wouldn't turn all the way over.

Now in full on freak out mode Barry felt like he was on the cusp of having a panic attack. He along with Damon pleaded for the car to start. The woman pulled her free arm from behind her back, something dangled from her hand. It took Damon a moment to realize it was the battery cables. As the fear bubbled up into his throat, he couldn't even react. His buddy looked on in horror. The man pounced out of the back seat, grabbed Damon under the chin with one arm, and plunged his knife into Damon's ear with the other. Damon shook violently a few times before going lifeless. Barry seized the opportunity to bail out of the car. He took off in a sprint into the wooded area next to the cemetery. He could hear the sounds of the child running and laughing close behind him.

Barry's legs throbbed and ached as he made his way down the embankment by the creek that ran behind the cemetery. Rats scurried around as he interrupted their feasting on a pile of fast food garbage. Barry lost his balance as he glanced back over his shoulder for his pursuers. He wiped out in the shallow muddy water. The man from the backseat crashed down upon him as he tried to get up. Barry fought back, trying to get away. He almost made it until the man grabbed him by his hair and forced his head under the water. Barry dug his hands into the mud as he pushed up with all his might. He lifted the man enough to break his hold on him. Barry jumped to his feet again and took off, running as fast as his body would carry him. He ran back up a less steep part of the bank and back into the dense wooded area. His knees gave out, and he collapsed to the ground, gasping for air next to a large tree. He looked down and even in the dark he could see leeches stuck to his body in various places. In disgust and horror he tried to swipe them off, to no avail. Distracted by the leeches he didn't notice the footsteps creep up behind him. Barry looked up in fear as the large man drove his blade down into his chest once, twice, three times, four, and passed out.

When he came to, he groggily looked down at his blood soaked clothes. Tied to the wrought iron bars of the area in the cemetery fenced off for the mother and child, he struggled. In his haze he noticed the three sets of feet a short distance in front of him.

"Look at me." The females voice commanded. Barry looked up the best he could. In front him stood his three assailants. The woman and child still wore their masks. The man stood tall wearing dark pants and a denim jacket with leather studded shoulders.

"The legend always lures someone in." The lady spoke again. "We will always protect our family, no one will desecrate our loved ones."

WELCOME TO COTTONWOOD CREEK

Barry tried to speak but no words would come out. He started to weep as he dropped his chin into chest, his consciousness wavering.

"Do it now, make him suffer." The woman ordered.

With the demand the man and the boy approached Barry. Without warning the man reached down with a pair of needle nose pliers and began to pull out his fingernails. The boy produced a Swiss army knife and started stabbing him over and over repeatedly in his legs. The man and child were enjoying themselves as laughter erupted from their bellies. Finally, the woman neared him. She knelt down in front of him and removed her mask.

She lifted Barry's face to look into his eyes, leaned forward, and kissed him. As she released the hold on his lips, a blade slid under his chin. Blood gurgled from Barry's mouth as he slumped forward in his restraints, his life fading to black.

ABOUT THE AUTHORS

DAVID OWAIN HUGHES

David Owain Hughes is a horror freak! He grew up on ninja, pirate and horror movies from the age of five, which helped rapidly instill in him a vivid imagination. When he grows up, he wishes to be a serial killer with a part-time job in women's lingerie...He's had multiple short stories published in various online magazines and anthologies, along with articles, reviews and interviews. He's written for This Is Horror, Blood Magazine, and Horror Geeks Magazine. He's the author of the popular novels "Walled In" (2014), "Wind-Up Toy" (2016), "Man-Eating Fucks" (2016), and "The Rack & Cue" (2017) along with his short story collections "White Walls and Straitjackets" (2015) and "Choice Cuts" (2015). He's also written three novellas – "Granville" (2016), "Wind-Up Toy: Broken Plaything & Chaos Rising" (2016).

His tales in this anthology were published by HellBound Books - all the stories appear in his collection 'Psychological Breakdown'.

https://www.facebook.com/DOHughesAuthor/?ref=hl

http://www.amazon.co.uk/David-Owain-Hughes/e/B00L708P2M/ref=sr_ntt_srch_lnk_3?qid=1458241417&sr=1-3

http://david-owain-hughes.wix.com/horrorwriter

https://www.goodreads.com/author/show/4877205.David_Owain_Hughes

https://twitter.com/DOHUGHES32

JONATHAN EDWARD ONDRASHEK

Jonathan Edward Ondrashek is an Operations supervisor by day and moonlights as a horror/dark fantasy writer and editor. He's the author of The Human-Undead War Trilogy (*Dark Intentions*, *Patriarch*, and *A Kingdom's Fall*). His short stories have appeared in numerous horror anthologies, including the highly acclaimed *Rejected for Content* and *VS: US vs UK Horror* series. He also co-edited *F*ck the Rules*, *What Goes Around,* and *Man Behind the Mask*, anthologies featuring work from established and new voices in the horror genre. If he isn't working at his day job, reading, editing, or writing, he's probably drinking beer and making his wife regret marrying a lunatic. Feel free to stalk him on social media.

   Website: www.jondrashek.com
   Facebook: www.facebook.com/JondrashekAuthor
   Twitter: @jondrashek
   Instagram: @jondrashek

MAXINE GREY

Since a young girl, Maxine escaped into a world of words and imagination with her obsessive love of books. Born in Newcastle-Upon-Tyne in the North East of England, she moved to Australia at the age of ten where eventually she had a successful career in advertising, copywriting, media and recruitment. Her favourite genres always being horror, crime and dark psychological fiction. She admits an obsession with True Crime also.

Returning to the UK in 2013, Maxine now resides in County Durham with her nineteen-year-old son and two very naughty Burmese cats. Booklover Catlady Publicity was born as a business in 2015 and quickly became popular as Maxine helped hundreds of authors, from new indie to household names with their book publicity. She is also a world ranked Book Reviewer and in the Top 500 Reviewers on Amazon UK devouring up to 300 books a year.

In 2017 she submitted her first short story for consideration for a horror anthology, rejected the first time but absorbed the second time into the dark humour/horror anthology Demonic Wildlife. Following this another story was published in Demonic Household in 2018. In 2019 Maxine will have two more short stories published in different horror anthologies including Demonic Carnival. All available on Amazon. Maxine Grey is the pen name of Maxine Groves.

She is currently working on a dark psychological thriller and has plans for a dark crime series set in the North East of England. In addition to this a non-fiction book is underway about Women on the Autism Spectrum and under a different pen name expect to see some dark romance/erotica. Big plans for a literary themed bookshop/café and gift shop is in project stage.

The deliberate plan to write short stories paid off with every story written now published. An anthology of her own short stories with the theme of women who have gone to the dark side will be published in 2019. Her passion is to encourage anyone with the dream to "just write it!" She is currently studying courses in Forensic Psychology and Criminology.

Maxine loves to interact with readers, other authors, budding writers and you can follow her and contact her via email or social media.

Facebook: www.facebook.com/maxinegreybooks

www.facebook.com/booklovercatlady

Twitter: www.twitter.com/maxinegreybooks

www.twitter.com/promotethatbook

Email: maxinegrey.writer@gmail.com

AARON THORTON

Aaron hails from Manhattan, KS, where he co-owns and operates Brew Bros Hops & Sprockets, a bicycle shop that sells homebrew supplies. Whenever he's not working, he enjoys writing, listening to soft hits from the eighties, taking moonlit strolls along the freeway, and leaving shit stains on the basins of his enemies' toilet bowls.

--

Brew Bros Hops & Sprockets
1110 Laramie
Manhattan, KS 66502
785.537.3737

CAITLIN GEER

Welcome Caitlin Geer. Rearview Mirror is Caitlin's first published project. She is a zombie lover at heart and fan of the horror genre. When she is not writing Caitlin is busy entertaining the masses by other means on The Wave 100.3 or 92.7 The Blast out of Wichita, Ks. If you would like to learn more about Caitlin or find out some of her many talents follow her on Twitter @radiocaitlin

THOMAS BAKER

Thomas is a lover of all things horror with a heavy emphasis on zombies, paranormal, and things of the slasher variety. He grew up convincing his mom to let him watch all the scary movies he could get his hands on. He aims to keep his writing fast paced and fun. He is best known for his co-written "Outbreak Series" with his good friend and writing partner Robert. The series has reached trilogy status with the titles "Safe Haven", "Purgatory" and "Dead Of Winter" You can follow him on his 6K Press page on both Facebook and Twitter to stay up to date on the latest shenanigans that are afoot! Be warned, some parental advisory required.

ROBERT WAGNER

Robert Wagner lives in the Kansas City area, is a husband, and a father of twin boys. He likes post apocalyptic stories, probably a little too much. Somehow he also fits in the time to write. A horror, science fiction and fantasy book fan since his teens, (which was a very long time ago) Robert hopes he can bring enjoyment to his readers like Fred Saberhagen, Michael Moorcock, Anne McCaffrey, J.R.R. Tolkien, Stephen King, and many other did for him. He's also a big video game enthusiast, since the days of the Atari 2600 (told you it was a long time ago.)You can find him at these places.

www.6kpress.com
www.facebook.com/6kpress
www.twitter.com/6k_press

Printed in Great Britain
by Amazon